The SILVER TREASURE

The SILVER TREASURE

MYTHS AND LEGENDS OF THE WORLD

GERALDINE McCAUGHREAN

Illustrated by
Bee Willey

MARGARET K. McELDERRY BOOKS

By the same author and illustrator

THE GOLDEN HOARD
MYTHS AND LEGENDS OF THE WORLD

FOR AILSA
If I could I would give you all the stories in the world
G.M.

FOR MY MOTHER
B.W.

MARGARET K. McELDERRY BOOKS
25 YEARS • 1972–1997

MARGARET K. McELDERRY BOOKS
An imprint of Simon & Schuster Children's Publishing Division
1230 Avenue of the Americas
New York, New York 10020

First published in London by Orion Children's Books
First United States Edition 1997

Book design by Dalia Hartman
The text of this book is set in Garland Light.
The illustrations were rendered in mixed media.

Printed in Italy
10 9 8 7 6 5 4 3 2 1
Library of Congress Catalog Card Number: 96-76845

ISBN 0-689-81322-8

Contents

THE SILVER-MINERS *1*
A legend from Bolivia

THE MEN IN THE MOON *6*
A myth from Kenya

DREAM JOURNEY *14*
A Maori myth

ROLAND AND HORN OLIVANT *20*
A legend from France

A QUESTION OF LIFE AND DEATH *27*
A Greek myth

THE HARP OF DAGDA *31*
An Irish myth

A NEST AND A WEB *38*
A legend from the Middle East

ASH *42*
A Native American myth of the Tlingit tribe

THE TOWER OF BABEL *51*
A Hebrew myth

SAINT CHRISTOPHER *53*
A European legend

GOD MOVES AWAY *57*
A myth from Togo

WILHELM TELL *60*
A Swiss legend

A HEART OF STONE *70*
A Greek myth

BABUSHKA *75*
A Russian legend

THE PIG GOES COURTING *81*
A Hawaiian myth

CAN KRISHNA DIE? *86*
An Indian legend

THE LIGHTHOUSE ON THE LAKE *91*
A Japanese legend

KING ARTHUR GIVES BACK HIS SWORD *98*
A Celtic legend

A BLOODTHIRSTY TALE *103*
A myth from Ancient Egypt

RIP VAN WINKLE *108*
An American legend

THE RAVEN AND THE MOON *114*
An Alaskan Merit myth

SIR PATRICK SPENS *118*
A Scottish legend

THE SALTCELLAR *121*
A Scandinavian myth

ABOUT THE STORIES *127*

The Silver-Miners

A LEGEND FROM BOLIVIA

WHEN THE SPANISH came to South America, they looked around them at the people, but saw only the gold bands on their arms, the silver rings in their ears. They looked at the great stepped temples, like stairways to Heaven, and saw no gods, but only the golden chalices and silver plates the priests held. When they looked at Bolivia, beautiful with holy green mountains, they saw only huge heaps of earth threaded with silver ore. They saw no beauty but in digging, gouging, tearing. They dug silver mines.

Worse. They did not even do the digging themselves, but forced the local people into a slavery of breaking and carrying rocks. The mountain Parichata, husband-mountain of Tata-Turqui, guardian of Potosí Town, was torn and pounded with picks and shovels, and his silver ripped out to feed Spanish greed.

1

"O Parichata, forgive us!" groaned the laborers, swinging their long picks as the midday sun scorched down on them. "O Parichata, grieve with us!" they sobbed as they staggered beneath huge baskets of rock. "O Parichata, husband of Tata-Turqui, guardian of Potosí Town, have pity on us! Would that you were made all of mud and had not a grain of silver in you, that you might stand at peace in the landscape, and we beside you!"

But the air was so full of the sound of whips that their prayers seemed to be cracked and broken by the lash in midair, and to fall to the ground without ever reaching the ears of the gods. Only the crawling beetles on the ground waved their long antennae and scuttled away.

Each evening, at the end of the day's work, Maro the mule-boy would lead his father's skinny mules up the mountain path to the mines. It was his job to ensure the animals were ready and waiting for the first loads of the following day. The Spaniards paid Maro's father nothing, and the animals were already half-dead with overwork. "But better they should drop in their tracks," his father said, "than that mothers and children should die carrying rocks for these slave drivers."

Suddenly, Maro heard ahead of him on the path the clatter of hooves. More donkeys? How very strange. He had thought his was the only team for miles around. And when the mules appeared, they quite took his breath away, for not only were they glossy, sleek, and fat, but coal-black in coat and mane. Huge panniers were strapped to both sides of their saddles.

The muleteer driving them wore a straw hat that cast his face into shadow despite a bright moon. "Out of the way, boy!" he shouted at Maro. "Clear the path! Go back or die!"

"I shall die if I don't do as the Spaniards tell me," said Maro, but the muleteer uttered such a fearsome roar that both Maro and his donkeys scampered off the path in terror, and the black mules clattered on downward, unhindered. Maro ran after all his animals, gathered up their lead-ropes, and led them back down to the edge of town.

But his curiosity got the better of him. He could not bear not to know what was happening to his beloved mountain, and going back alone, on silent, bare feet, he hid himself beside the path and watched all night.

He saw, under the moonlight, how the chalky path was alive with insect life. Whole swarms of gleaming longicorn beetles, bugs, and mud-rollers were crawling upwards. Every beetle on Parichata seemed to be closing in on the silver mines.

Rank by rank, the beetles reached the mine workings — where the trees were all felled, the boulders smashed, the flowers uprooted, and the mountain's flesh cut to its very bones of silver. There, the Indian in the straw hat was waiting. He touched each beetle with his muleteer's goad, and rolled it onto its glossy back.

But when they rolled back again onto their feet, the feet they stood on were hooves, the legs they straightened were hairy, and their bodies and heads were those of fully grown handsome mules. In place of their antennae were long pink-lined ears, and over their backs the muleteer hung panniers of woven wickerwork.

Out of the mountain flowed molten silver. It spouted and spurted in

fountains and springs, directly into the panniers, and there solidified into shining ingots. With both panniers full, each mule turned down the mountain path and came clumping past Maro's hiding place before disappearing into the black distance, leaving only the echo of hooves clip-clopping among the rocks.

The Spaniards arrived next morning, eager and anxious for a new day's loot. Their weary slaves rolled miserably out of bed and crawled up the pocked and scarred mountainside. They found (to their amazement) that there was no silver to mine.

The Spaniards looked — oh, how they looked! — sinking new drill holes, scrambling down every crevice, peeling back the grass as though they would flay the mountain. But they could find no trace of silver, not the merest grain, not the tiniest glitter. It was as if all Parichata's silver bones had been cut out.

"You won't find any." Maro spoke up, standing between the muzzles of his father's mules. His neighbors looked around at him in astonishment. The Spaniards scowled. "Parichata took pity on us last night. He gave away his silver for the sake of the people." And Maro went on to tell them how every beetle had been turned into a mule and had carried away the precious ore. The Spanish only snorted with disbelief, but the people of Potosí Town looked down at the ground and saw no beetles, no, not so much as a single leather beetle creeping to and fro.

No one ever discovered where the beetle-mules took their treasure of silver. Perhaps they gave it into the safekeeping of Tata-Turqui, wife-mountain of Parichata, or perhaps they carried it into the valleys, to some secret treasure-house. But though the Spaniards raged and threatened, they had, in the end, to quit Potosí and seek their riches elsewhere.

The scars on the face of Parichata soon healed. Spring brought its yearly treasure of seeds, berries, flowers, and sapling trees. And after morning had dropped its dew on every spider's web and leaf and bending blade of grass, Parichata was not entirely without a gleam of silver in the early dawn.

The Men in the Moon

A MYTH FROM KENYA

"MURILAY, come here! Murilay, don't do that! Murilay, I've told you before! Murilay, just wait till your father comes home!"

Murilay hunched his shoulders and slunk out of doors. He could hear his mother's shrill voice still scolding inside the hut, her words hunting after him like stinging red ants.

A wooden stool stood beside the door — the carved seat where Murilay's father liked to sit in the evenings and watch the huge sun shimmer and ripple as it set, and the clean sharp-edged rising moon cut its way like a sickle through the last stems of cloud and the rain of stars. "We may have nothing," Murilay's father liked to say, pointing at the sky with his knurled and gnarled old walking stick, "but we are as rich in stars as the next man."

Murilay liked to watch the sunset, too, but his mother never let him sit

6

down for long enough. "Eat your supper, Murilay! Wash your face, Murilay! Go to bed, Murilay, and get up a better boy. The boys in the moon never disobey their mother. The boys in the moon always do as they're told. The boys in the moon aren't lazy, idle, good-for-nothing boys like you!"

Murilay seized his chance now to sit, for once, upon his father's stool. "The boys in the moon are lucky," he said out loud. "I wish I could be up there in the peace and quiet."

The stool rocked, the stool swayed, the stool reared up like a horse, and it was all Murilay could do not to tumble off. The stool took a practice leap into the branches of a nearby tree, and balanced there, quivering with pent-up magic.

Murilay was excited. "Up, stool, up!" he said. "Up to the moon!"

The stool rose further up, resting at intervals on a cloudbank, a ledge of rainbow. Finally, the blue sky gave way to the blackness of space, and Murilay flew on his stool as far as the moon, where he landed in a pleasant landscape yellow with moon-bleached grass.

A group of men came by, driving cows ahead of them. They cast a wary eye over the boy sitting on a stool in the middle of nowhere.

"Please, gentlemen," Murilay asked politely, "can you direct me to the Chief of the Moon People?"

They knew at once he was a stranger, and grinned in a way not entirely friendly. "You want directions? You earn them. You work for us for a month."

So Murilay worked for the men, grooming their cows and fetching water from the deep wells of the moon. His mother's nagging had accustomed Murilay to worse than anything these men could inflict, and he was not unhappy. Time only hung heavily because the food was so *bad*. At the end of each day the cowherds gave him stone-cold porridge, uncooked and indigestible. He might have understood, if they had eaten differently — but they ate the same themselves!

"I have worked one month for you. Now tell me, gentlemen, where I may find the Chief of the Moon People." The cowherds gave a variety of grunts and pointed out a path. Murilay ran down it before they could change their minds.

The path did indeed bring him to the village of the Moon Chief. It was a dark, dismal place, and very cold. The people huddled under blankets in the doorways of their huts, crunching nuts between broken teeth or sipping cold porridge. The Chief himself sat on a carved wooden chair watching the earth rise, like a green-and-blue duck egg, alongside a sprinkling of stars. The first remark he made to Murilay was, "We may not have much to call our own, stranger, but we are as rich in stars as the next village." He waved in one fist a giant turkey wing still stubbly from plucking, and completely raw.

When he offered Murilay something to eat, a servant brought the meat of a moon rabbit; that, too, dripped blood.

"Eat, eat, young man! Don't stand on ceremony! You must be very hungry if you've traveled all the way from earth and done a month's work as well!"

"The gods forbid that I should offend your highness," said Murilay, "and I realize that the fault is all mine, but I am accustomed to eating my food . . . how can I say this? . . . cooked."

"Cooked? How 'cooked'? What does it mean?" said the Chief, scowling over his turkey wing.

"With fire," said Murilay.

"Fire? And what's that?"

The Chief's wives were glaring at Murilay from under the blankets, dark eyes enveloped in wool and bad temper. Murilay began to see the moon in quite a new light. He searched about for two flints, pulled a tuft of hair from his head for kindling, and — to the great astonishment of the whole tribe — struck a spark.

He fanned it to a flame, fed it with wood, and, looking about for food to cook, took the turkey drumstick from the Chief's hand. Warrior body-guards lifted their spears menacingly. But Murilay persevered in cooking the turkey on the fire, while the People of the Moon were busy discovering the delights of warmth. They crept from under their blankets. They gazed round-eyed at the leaping fire, and burned themselves trying to pick it up.

"To think that my mother thought these folk were far above us!" thought

Murilay, but kept the thought to himself.

When the Chief of the Moon tasted his roast turkey, he at once offered Murilay all his daughters as wives.

Murilay had not been planning to marry so young, but the prospect of marrying seven princesses in one day quite changed his outlook. Gifts of cattle and sheep followed the marriage, and by nightfall, Murilay was proclaimed the greatest magician in the Realm of Stars.

While Murilay grew to manhood, the People of the Moon prospered as they had never done before. By the time he had a hut and a family of children, his wealth was second only to the Chief's.

But sometimes, when he sat on his father's wooden stool and watched the earth rising, he longed to see, from earth, the moon cut cleanly through the last stems of evening cloud. He wanted to see his father again and hear the crows in the treetops at dusk, as shrill as his mother.

He decided to go back, but going was not as simple as coming. He might fly back on his magic stool, as easily as the birds hopped between earth and moon, but he had his wives and cows and children and sheep to think of. All on one stool, they would find the journey hugely overcrowded. There was a place where the moon dipped down and the earth sloped up, and a causeway joined the two. But it would be a difficult, dangerous journey to make. So he sent word ahead, by way of the mockingbird, telling his family to meet him halfway and help with the cattle.

"Muri-i-i-lay! Muri-i-i-lay! Home soon, home soon!" squawked the mockingbird, and gave a burst of brash, brittle laughter. "Meet him halfway to the moon!"

Murilay's father picked up a stone and threw it. "Wicked bird! Do you want to break my heart with your lies? My Murilay is dead these seven years!"

"Muri-i-i-lay be home soon!" cackled the bird. But Murilay's mother came after it with a broom, and cursed it with a dozen curses for lying about her poor dead son. The mockingbird flew back to the moon and explained the problem to Murilay.

"You lazy, idle, good-for-nothing, laze-in-the-sun-all-day, lying bird!" exclaimed Murilay. "You never even went there! My parents would never give me up for dead, just because I disappeared for a few years!"

The poor mockingbird flew back down to earth and swooped low over the house of Murilay's parents. It snatched the knurled and gnarled walking stick out of the old man's hand. The old man stood up, but the bird flew out of reach of his old, weak hands. He watched until the bird flew out of sight of his old, weak eyes.

Then Murilay had to accept that he must make the journey all by himself, and set off for earth with his wives and children and cattle and sheep, skidding down the slopes of moon-white scree.

The cattle slid on their hocks, Murilay skidded on his heels, the white moon-dust filling his hair and clogging his throat. A trail of milk, white as moonlight, dripped from the udders of the milk cows. Murilay's wives and children soon grew tired and rode on the backs of the cows.

Then Murilay grew weary, too, and feared he could go no further. When he reached the causeway joining the moon to the earth, he sat down with his head between his knees and wept. For the causeway passed over a bottomless chasm so terrifying that Murilay dared not go one step across it. He was already dizzy with weariness, and his courage was fading fast.

"I will carry you across."

"Who said that?"

"I did," said the bull. "I'll carry you over, if you promise my reward won't be the butcher's knife. I've seen what your fire does to meat, and I daresay beef is dear to you People of Earth."

"I promise I shall never again eat red meat, if you will carry me over the Ravine of Nothingness," vowed Murilay.

So the bull took Murilay on its back, and, as surefooted as any mountain goat, tripped across the knife-edge-narrow isthmus to the great meadows of Africa.

That evening, Murilay's father and mother sat on the ground outside their hut. (The stool which had once stood there was gone.) They watched the sun set — saw its big mottled face dip beneath the fumes of dusk and waver like the thinnest wafer of gold leaf. Then the moon rose, clean and sharp-edged as a scythe, and cut its way through the last stems of evening cloud and the rain of stars.

"I would give every star in the sky to see my son again," said the old man to his wife, and his wife said, "So would I."

Out of the darkness came the lowing of a hundred cattle, and off the plain came a herd of moon-white cows led by a coppery bull. Riding on the bull was Murilay, their long-lost son, as rich as the richest, as fit as the fittest, as happy as the happiest, pointing at the stars with a knurled and gnarled stick and singing a song he had learned on the moon.

Dream Journey

A MAORI MYTH

THERE WAS ONCE a great chieftain named Kahakura whose mind was as wide as the plain and whose dreams were as bright as sunshine. One night, a dream shone on his sleep that was almost too dazzling to comprehend, but it filled him with feelings of great hope and excitement. "Go north," said the voice in his dream. "Go north, and I will show you the shape of happiness.

"Go alone, without a sound,
Like the shadow of a bird
Passing over broken ground,
Or flies' flicker. Be not heard
More than time passing."

Kahakura was so thrilled by his dream that he got up at once and ran down to the beach to tell his people. The young men of his tribe stood about, balanced precariously on the seaside rocks, aiming spears at the fish in the water. They would throw, jump in, retrieve their spears, and begin again. Their catch lay on the shore — a couple of bass and a flatfish.

"I must go away! I've dreamed a dream," announced Kahakura. "I've seen a vision. I've been made a promise by the gods! Stay here and wait: I'm going north to fetch the gift the gods have promised us!"

The young men stood on one leg and stared at him openmouthed. Go away? Leave them without a chief and go north into hostile country? Not if they could help it.

"We'll come with you!" they said, jumping down into the surf. "We'll all go!" They wanted neither to miss out on the adventure nor to see their chief disappear over the horizon without knowing when or if he would return. So, although Kahakura insisted he must go alone, they dogged his footsteps around the settlement and stuck as fast to him as his own shadow. Kahakura began to think he might not be able to do as his dream instructed: his own people would stop him from making whatever marvelous discovery awaited him in the north.

One evening, when the whole village was dancing, the music loud, and the singing cacophonous, Kahakura backed away into the surrounding darkness. He cast a last fond look at his people dancing in a pool of firelight, then turned and began to run — northward.

For many days, he trekked through the provinces of tribes whose warriors would have speared him as eagerly as fishermen spearing a fish. But Kahakura wove his way through the gray tassels at either end of day, when the ground is carpeted neither with light nor dark.

At long last, he came to a country called Rangiaowhia, fluffy with white flax and fringed with yellow sand. He first glimpsed the sea in the early morning. It seemed to Kahakura that the moon, in leaving the sky, must have fallen and smashed. For the sea was silver with sparkling lozenges of metallic light. Then the water began to rattle and leap, to explode with fish, such crowds of them that they shouldered each other out of the water to somersault in the surf. A feast of fish! Kahakura's first instinct was to race into the surf and gather them up in armfuls — but instead, he hid himself. He was not first on the scene. Someone was already busy catching the fish.

The fishermen were the frail, slender, tiny Sea People — a tribe who lived among the ocean waves and came ashore only as often as the Land People put out to sea. Kahakura had heard tell of them, and now here they were — in front of his very eyes — fishing. And not with spears!

Looking once more at the multitude of fish in the bay, Kahakura saw that they were being hauled in and harvested in a giant bag — a spider's web of woven thread, delicate as hair yet strong as sinew. When the mouth of the bag was closed, inside it were trapped not one fish or two, but one or two *thousand!*

Kahakura stared. "*This* is what I was sent here to see," he thought. "A way of catching fish that will feed my tribe for all time! As long as the sea runs and fish run in the sea, we'll never be hungry again! I must take that bag home with me, to copy how it is made."

From his hiding place, Kahakura watched the Sea People struggle. Though they were pretty, with their yellow hair and pale, smooth skins, they were a puny race, narrow-chested, thin-shanked, with pinched moonish faces. It took twenty men to land the catch, whereas Kahakura could have done it with a couple of friends.

The work done, the young men lay about exhausted among their canoes, while their blond women gutted and cleaned the fish. A flock of gulls gathered to eat the offal, and frightened the Sea People's tiny children.

Apart from the other women sat a girl quite different from the rest. She had the task of mending the net. Children sat about her feet, laughing at

the stories and jokes she told them, but the other women sat with their
backs turned, and threw her not so much as a civil word. Perhaps it was
her beauty that made them resent her. Perhaps it was her formidable size
that made the men equally unkind. Taller than the tallest fishermen, she
had hips like the curving bole of a tree, and arms strong enough to carry
a family of children. Her clever hands wove and knotted flaxen thread
into the holes where the net had torn. Kahakura was so entranced by the
sight of her and her quick, darting fingers that he almost forgot why the
gods had sent him to Rangiaowhia.

The net!

He jumped up from his hiding place, and as his head rose above the
bushes, he realized he had not even thought what to say, or how to
come by the precious net that now lay stretched at the girl's feet. He had
nothing to trade for it, no weapon to fight with for it, and the language
of the Sea People was strange to him. So when they caught sight of him,

he spoke with a great loud voice — as people do to make foreigners understand them.

"I am Kahakura of the Maori People! I dreamed a dream and I saw a vision . . . Wait, don't go!"

The Sea People took one look at his towering frame, huge shoulders, broad chest. Then mothers snatched up their children and threw them into the canoes, jumping in after them. The men plunged into the surf and dragged the canoes out to sea.

The big yellow-haired girl took two steps from her seat and fell, her feet tangled in the net she had been mending. Her basket of threads and tools was spilled on the ground. For a moment, Kahakura thought to bundle her up in the net like a giant tuna and sling her over his back. He had to have her for his wife, to stroke that golden hair, and watch her bounce his children on her knee.

But the thought came to him — as clearly as the dream had come to him in sleeping — that a man does not take a wife in the same way as a fisherman takes a tuna. So he stood just where he was, and allowed her to untangle her feet and get up.

She ran a few steps toward the sea, saw her tribe and family paddling away, abandoning her, but she did not cry out. She looked back to where Kahakura stood wearing a crooked, uncertain smile. He gathered up the spilled tools and thread and handed the basket back to her. "It is as the gods wish, or my eyes would not have seen you," he said. And she seemed to understand.

So Kahakura took home to his tribe the amazing secret of fishing nets — how they are used and how they are made. And he took home, too, a wife with golden hair and hips curved like the bole of a flourishing tree, and strong arms destined to hold a family of children. As long as the sea runs and the fish run in the sea, the Maori People will never go hungry for fish, nor empty of love. It is as the gods wish.

Roland and
Horn Olivant

A LEGEND FROM FRANCE

THE KNIGHTS of Charlemagne were like the spring flowers that brighten fields as far as the eye can see. Resplendent with flapping pennons and banners of purple silk, the army prinked its way on high-prancing horses over the faces of their fallen enemy, the Saracens; its minstrels outsang the evening birds. Saddlecloths swept the ground like the skirts of the women waiting at home for the knights of Charlemagne, the finest men in all the world.

Even in retreat they were magnificent. They carried their wounds like the red rosettes of victory, and they died with a joke and a prayer. The army of Charlemagne was like the spring that covers the fields in flowers … but the Saracens were like the locusts that strip fields bare. Though the Emperor Charlemagne had conquered most of the world, the Saracens denied him the realms of Spain. Their troops massed to turn him back, as tightly packed as bricks in a wall. In the end, there was no more purpose to be served in throwing good men against such a wall to see them break, and Charlemagne withdrew. His knights were the finest in all the world, and the finest of them all was Roland.

"Sir Roland, my friend and pride of my knights," said Charlemagne, "command the rearguard, I beg you, and shelter the wounded and the weary from attack as we retreat."

"I shall, my lord — if we really must leave Spain unconquered."

"Better to withdraw and come back another day than grant the enemy our blood to walk in and our shields to decorate their halls . . . Do you have Olivant with you?"

Sir Roland nodded and pointed to his horse. Hung by a scarlet cord from his saddle was a huge horn — the tusk of an elephant, carved by Roland's own hand, reamed and bored with fire and hot steel. No one but Roland could blow it, and there was no sound like the shriek of Horn Olivant. "If you need reinforcements," said the Emperor, "sound Olivant, and I shall turn back to help you."

Roland, in his pride, bridled a little, and his cheeks flushed. "I shall summon you, my lord, if I prove unequal to my task."

The army began to move. Like a frozen river thawed by spring, it moved between the craggy mountain passes. First came Charlemagne with his princes, dukes and earls; then his knights, squires, and foot-soldiers; next the wagons and the wagonboys, the armorers, farriers, and fletchers; the machinery and engines of war. After came the dead, fetched out of battle by their friends for decent burial in a Christian land; and behind them, moving with painful slowness, came the wounded and the sick, wearing bloodstained banners for blankets and marching in silence, without breath enough for song.

Behind them came the troops of Roland, half-turned in their saddles to watch for pursuers.

"Charlemagne leaving Spain? By the god I serve, he shall not!" declared the great Sultan in his marble court. "Pursue him with sword and arrow and let not one man live who has offended me by setting foot in Spain! No, when your work is done let not two letters of that filthy name hang together: *Charlemagne!*"

At Roncesvalles it happened. The Saracens came down like wolves upon a flock of sheep. When Roland saw the dust raised by their horses' hooves, he wheeled his knights about and deployed them as a blockade across the path. To shield the retreating column, Roland made a wall of men to stop the Saracen rout.

"We shall be the reef on which they founder!" he shouted to his men, and the sight of his great warhorse, prancing from end to end of the human wall, put heart into his battalion and fired them with resolve. "Ours is the honor of saving Charlemagne's army, that he may go on to win new victories! Ours is the honor of doing our duty! Let us leave the Saracens with one last taste of our mettle! Let us write one last page of history!"

And it seemed as though that page would be written in gold. For five tides of Saracens broke against the reef of Frankish knights, but it held fast, and they could not break through. Like summer flies the Saracens fell, while the Frankish shields held firm, edge to edge — a palisade painted with heraldic beasts. At long last, the Saracens withdrew, and the weary knights drew breath and congratulated one another on their daring and skill.

Then five more battalions of Saracens appeared over the rocky horizon.

So the page of history was to be written in blood, after all. As the five tides broke against the Frankish reef, soldiers too weary any longer to lift a sword were trampled down. Knights wounded in the first onslaught found their limbs too cold to raise lance or axe, and fell beneath Saracen swords. When at last the tenth battalion was driven off, the splendor of Charlemagne's rearguard was as tattered as a wind-frayed banner. Still, the wall had held. The column of wounded and sick crept away around distant bends in the mountain track.

"The day is ours, and all the honor!" cried Roland exultantly. "I did not sound Horn Olivant, for we alone did what was asked of us!" He rose proudly in his stirrups.

That was when he glimpsed the dust of five battalions more.

"Sound the horn now, my lord!" exclaimed his sergeant. "Signal the Emperor that we are outnumbered!"

"And lose the honor of the day? Plead for help? No! Olivant shall not speak today! Not while I have power to lift my sword, and men around me who are Franks!"

So the Saracen battalions broke over the reef of Frankish knights and swept many away. Horses clad in Frankish colors lay dead on top of their dead riders, and fallen shields bossed the ground.

Each man spent his life dearly, and took ten Saracen souls with him to the gates of death. Even so, when the third onslaught fell back, nothing more was left of Roland's defensive wall than a knot of fifty exhausted men.

"We have turned them! We have finished them!" exclaimed Roland, crimson from head to foot in the blood of his enemies.

As one man, the fifty lay down with a crash of buckled armor. They were too weary to raise a cheer. They had seen too many friends die to glory in their survival. A dozen vultures hopped and crouched within arm's reach, but no one had strength to shoo them away. Over the distant mountain ridges, the last of the column of retreating Frankish wounded moved out of sight. Roland watched them disappear with satisfaction.

Turning back, he saw, by the light of the low sun, another five battalions of Saracens closing in fast. Their numbers were as vast as the waves in the sea. They would wash over Roland's rearguard like the ocean over a handful of pebbles.

Fifty men looked at him with despair in their eyes. Fifty swords stabbed the ground, as the knights of Roland dragged themselves painfully to their feet once more.

Only then did Roland reach for his ivory horn. He placed it to his lips, and prayed for breath enough to blow it. He summoned the breath from the four winds, and he blew till his eyes and ears bled.

Olivant gave a blast which froze the Saracen horses in their tracks. Overhead in the sky, birds stricken by the note fell dead onto the helms of the advancing Moors. Elephants bellowed on the dusty plains of Africa, as if stirred by a memory. Boulders rolled and shattered, and the clodded mud shivered into sandy grains.

Roland's horse died beneath him, its great heart shrunk by the terrible noise. And Horn Olivant, sounded a thousand times in victory, cracked and split in sounding defeat.

Twenty miles away, Charlemagne put his hands to his ears at the sound. He knew Horn Olivant as well as the cry of his own baby son, as well as the echo of his own voice.

"Roland needs us!" he told his princes and dukes, his earls and knights.

They rode back through the brightly clothed squires, past the muddy foot soldiers, through the feathered ranks of archers, past the wagons and wagonboys. Their frenzied gallop startled the armorers and farriers, shook the machines and engines of war. The dead men slung across their saddles

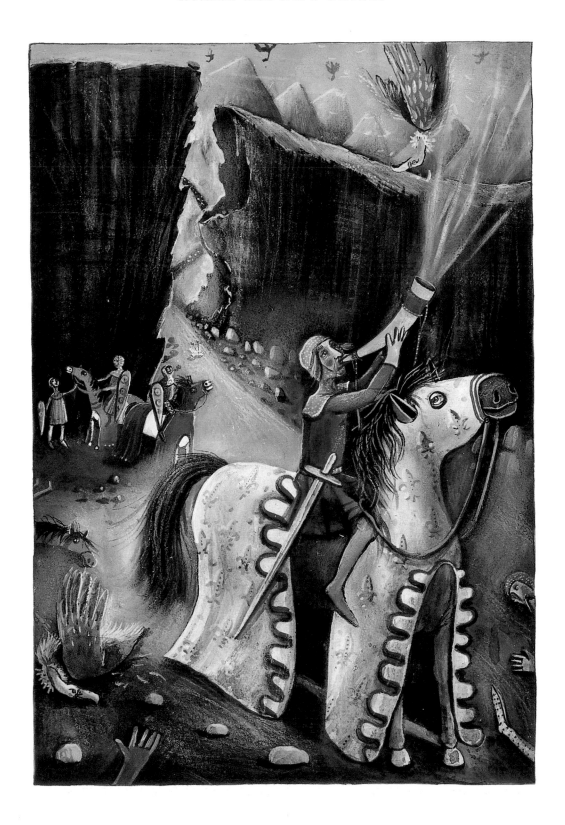

all but woke. The wounded and the sick shuffled aside to make room, for they too had heard the cry of Horn Olivant and knew that Roland was in need of help.

Too late did Charlemagne return to Roncesvalles. Too late did he counter the last Saracen attack. One hundred thousand of the enemy had finally overwhelmed the troops of Roland, and the finest of the Frankish chivalry lay like a field of flowers killed by frost.

Roland himself lay face up to the sky, beside him Horn Olivant, like a crescent moon cradling the sun. Across his legs lay a Saracen banner, token of respect from one race of knights to another. At the sight of it, Charlemagne wept. "O proud, proud Roland! Why did you wait so long to sound your horn?" asked the Emperor of his finest knight. But Roland said nothing in reply. The lips that had sounded Horn Olivant were silent now, and pale as ivory.

A Question of Life and Death

A GREEK MYTH

THE PEOPLE of Thebes grew lazy and selfish, and begrudged the things they had once given to the gods. They visited the temple of the sun god Apollo less and less often, left smaller and smaller offerings on the altar. One day, when he found nothing but a half-eaten apple and a sardine where once there had been whole carcasses of beef, whole sheaves of flowers, he considered the time had come to remind Thebes of its duties to the gods. He sent a monster, a creature of hideous grace, of grotesque magnificence, to devour anyone who set foot outside the town.

The Sphinx — part woman, part lion, part eagle — made her lair above the main highway out of Thebes, couched on a ledge of rock. Whenever a traveler passed by, down she would leap, waving her lion's tail. The traveler, stricken with wonder as much as fear, would gaze up at the tumbling mane of black and gold fur, the soulful features, the gigantic wings raising the Sphinx rampant off the ground. Her shadow cast the whole valley into gloom.

"Answer me this riddle," she would demand, in a voice as big as doom. "Which animal has four legs in the morning, two in the afternoon, three in the evening, and is weakest when it has most?"

It was the kind of teaser that might go around at a party, or to pass the time on a journey. And yet no one who trod that road out of Thebes thought the riddle a small or trivial joke. It was a question of life or death. For when they guessed wrongly, the Sphinx tore them cloth from clothes, hair from head, limb from trunk, body from soul, and ate each piece.

Soon no one dared come to Thebes and no one dared leave. The Council sat to discuss the answer to the riddle. The townspeople huddled on street corners, their only conversation the Riddle of the Sphinx. Rewards were offered — the throne of Thebes and the hand of the newly widowed queen in marriage — and people reckless or penniless or cocksure enough risked answering the Sphinx's riddle.

"Which animal has four legs in the morning, two in the afternoon, three in the evening, and is weakest when it has most?"

"A giraffe!"

"A circus horse!"

"One of the constellations!"

No one returned to claim their reward.

"A centipede!"

"One of the gods!"

"A cockatrice!"

No one returned.

Then along came Oedipus. He approached Thebes one green morning — and was met by the Sphinx.

"Which animal has four legs in the morning, two in the afternoon, three in the evening, and is weakest when it has most?"

Oedipus shielded his eyes and looked up at the Sphinx, a woman of sumptuous beauty imprisoned in the body of a lion and given only wings to solace her. "You are only a lion, and though the lion is called King of the Beasts, truly it is not: Man is that. You are only an eagle, and though you may fly high over the earth, you do not rule it: Man does that. You are only a woman, and though you may have had men love, hate, or fear you, you are powerless: Man will always oppress you."

"Answer my riddle!" demanded the Sphinx in a voice as terrible as fate.

"I already have. A man crawls on all fours when he's a baby, on two when he's grown, and leans on a stick in his old age, when he's frail and toothless. 'Man' is the answer to your riddle, and Oedipus is the man who answered it."

At that, the Sphinx gave a scream, like an eagle falling, like a lion caught in a trap, like a woman vexed to the point of desperation. She pounced at Oedipus — over Oedipus — clearing his head with her lion's leap. Over the brink of a gaping ravine she leaped. Her wings opened no more than a book riffling its torn pages, for she had chosen to die on the rocks below.

Thebes whooped with joy, opened its gates once more, and made Oedipus King. Once again they made sacrifices to Apollo and the gods who lived on Mount Olympus. People hardly bothered to remember the answer to the riddle, though they never forgot the Sphinx. Perhaps the true Riddle of the Sphinx is not what she asked, but why she asked it, and why the right answer drove her to such despair.

The Harp of Dagda

AN IRISH MYTH

THEY CAME from the four great cities in the sky — from Falias and Gorias, Finias and Murias. They had studied every kind of knowledge at the feet of the cities' Four Wise Kings, but their destiny was to live on earth a while, a tribe like any other. So they came riding down on the wind, hidden by magic clouds, and the home they chose — for were they not the wisest of the wise? — was Ireland. Their chieftain was Dagda, and they were like giant gods to the wild men of the bogs and peat lakes. They were the Good Men, the Dananns.

With them they brought the greatest treasures from each of the four celestial cities: a stone from Falias, a sword from Gorias, a spear from Finias, and, from Murias, the bottomless cauldron.

Even in times of famine, Dagda's Magic Cauldron was always full of meaty soup, or porridge threaded with golden honey, and no matter how many hungry people dipped in their spoons, it was never emptied, never scraped clean to the iron studs of its bulging belly. No wonder they clamored to make Dagda King of Ireland, too.

The Magic Stone was placed beneath the throne, and when Dagda seated himself, it roared like a lion, as if to say, "You have chosen aright. This is the true King." No king was chosen afterwards unless the stone shouted for him.

In battle the Magic Spear felled twenty men each time it was thrown, and the Magic Sword melted whole ranks of men where they stood.

But greater still than all these treasures were Dagda's harp and the harpist who played it to him at the glimmering fireside. For men can fight their battles with bare hands if need be, and tighten their belts when they are hungry. But no civilized man can live without music and song.

Even the barbarian, spitting into the straw of his squalid hut, wants music to soothe him at the end of a long day's cruelty. That is why the King of the Fomorians set his heart on having the harp of Dagda.

Nine winged Fomorian warriors from a neighboring tribe flew down on the castle of the Dananns, like skuas mobbing the snowy gulls on the cliffs of Tyree. Shrieking and swooping, they seized the harpist by his curly hair and lifted both him and his harp high into a stormy sky. The

Dananns, rushing to the doorway, shaking their swords at the diminishing shapes in the wild sky, felt rain fall in their faces like the notes of a lament.

"This time the Fomorians have flown one league too far into the realms of wickedness," said Dagda, his head brushing the roofbeams, his cloak extinguishing the fire. "Come, Men of the Good, and we shall get back the harp and the harpist of Dagda!"

"Shall we strike them dead with the Magic Spear of Finias?"

"Shall we cut them in pieces with the Magic Sword?"

Dagda considered, and upon consideration dropped his voice to a murmur. "No, children, no. For the harp has soul enough to yearn for its home, and the Fomorians have too little soul to know the value of what they have. There will be no need to spill blood."

Three men only, Dagda, Lugh, and Ogma the Warrior, traveled to the Fomorian settlement. It took them some time, for they did not fly, but patiently picked their way over bog and heath, sheep track and stony stream, till they saw a crooked pall of smoke rising from a crooked roof. The banqueting hall of the Fomorians was crammed with noise, but none was harp music. For the harp refused to sound and the harpist refused to play it, and no Fomorian had the art of making music. The King, after an outburst of spleen, had hung the harp, along with his other hunting trophies, high on the wall.

When he saw the gigantic Dagda filling the doorway of the banqueting hall, he rubbed his smoke-reddened eyes and grinned. "Come in! Come in!" he said, thinking to humiliate the Dananns still more with condescending shows of hospitality. "Cooks! Prepare a bite for the great Dagda. You know what an appetite the man has!"

Three men with shovels set about digging a pit in the floor, a trough big enough to hold a horse. Then the cooks brought cauldrons full of porridge and vats full of milk, and slopped them into the pit until a steaming pond lay at Dagda's feet, looking more like a bath than a meal.

"Most kind," said Dagda, graciously inclining his head. He pulled from his belt a spoon, or rather a ladle, its bowl so big that a man and woman could have cheerfully gone to bed in it and not fallen out till morning. In a matter of half a dozen spoonfuls, the porridge was gone, though Dagda stayed to scrape round the hole, supplementing his meal with a spoonful or two of gravel and earth.

While the Fomorians sat spellbound by this massive feat of eating, Dagda's eyes searched the smoky hall till they lit on the harp. Under his breath he began to say,

> "O come, my orchard of notes,
> Strung with the four seasons of sound.
> Come, you breath of spring,
> you heat of summer,
> you colors of autumn,
> you stillness of winter.
> Come, you bed of sweet sleep!
> Come, you square for dancing!
> Come, you weft of woven stories!
> Come, you web of captured dreams!
> Come, you magic, mouthless, marvelous, musical man of mine!"

The harp sprang from the wall and plunged like a fish eagle. It cracked against the skulls of the nine Fomorians who had raided the castle of Dagda, and their black wings sagged around them, moulting in the moment of death. Then it settled in the arms of Dagda, as gentle as Noah's dove returning to the ark.

As the room erupted into chaos, the Fomorian men diving for their swords, the women shrieking with terror, Dagda touched the strings of his harp and began to play — a hearty, happy tune. He smiled as he did so, and the harpist, who had crept to his feet, smiled too. But the Fomorians did more than smile. They began to laugh! They could not help it. Their shoulders jigged and their big bellies quaked while they laughed just as though they had heard the funniest of jokes.

They held their sides and dabbed their eyes, and those who had half

risen to kill the Dananns where they stood rolled across the table in paroxysms of helpless laughter.

Dagda passed the harp to his son Ogma, who played in a different key — a sad, lilting lament like the grief of a dying swan. The laughing Fomorians, like children at bedtime who have overexcited themselves, burst into sudden hysterical tears. Their eyes streamed and their mouths gaped open, wailing and weeping till the dirty floor was slippery with tears.

Then Ogma handed the harp to its harpist, who cradled it like a newborn baby and bent his head, low and loving, over the web of strings. The weeping Fomorians, despite their uncontrollable grief, had turned over the table and were starting to throw aside the stools to lay hands on the Dananns. Some had drawn swords, others spears that they raised overhead, preparing to impale the Good Men against the door.

But when the harpist began to play, the foremost spear-wielder halted on one foot and leaned backwards. His wailing mouth stretched wider still into a monumental yawn. Then he keeled over backward like a felled tree. Drunk with sudden sleepiness, the rest of the Fomorians reeled about, cannoning into one another and tumbling to the floor. Some slept propped in the corners, and one hung over the back of a chair.

The King simply rolled out of his throne and into the dogs' basket, where the hounds licked him curiously.

"Until we meet on the battlefield!" said Dagda to the sleeping Fomorians. "For such is our fate." Then he and his warriors closed the great doors softly behind them. The sound of snoring followed them all the way back to their castle.

The death of days and the tides of time wrought a change in the men called Good. When the world grew old and sour and villainous, like the Fomorians, the tribe of Good diminished — oh, not in wisdom or skill, but in actual physical stature. They shrank, just as the goodness of the world shrank, and changed their dwelling place once again, from earth to the places beneath the earth. They lived in the green mounds of the lonely places and changed — as the grub changes to a butterfly — into the fairies of Ireland.

And they took with them their treasures: the sword, the cauldron, the spear — all but the Magic Stone. Most certainly, they took Dagda's harp. That is why, sometimes, you may see a man, all alone and quite without cause, suddenly laugh out loud, or weep into his sleeve, or sit down be- neath a tree on a grassy mound and fall asleep with the ease of a child. He has heard the music, you see, coming from underground.

A Nest and a Web

AT FIRST, when Muhammad preached, they said he was mad. But that is not uncommon in the experience of prophets. When his words began to be believed, then he was in far greater danger.

For Muhammad the prophet lived in Mecca, city of the idol-makers, who had charge of the house of the gods and made their money selling idols. In those days, the house of the gods in Mecca held three hundred and sixty idols depicting the gods of a multitude of different religions. People came from all over the pagan world to worship this god or that goddess, and there was a great deal of money to be made from selling them goods and mementos of their pilgrimage.

But Muhammad spoke of only one God. "Smash the pagan idols, empty God's house of them. Allah is the one, the only God."

Now Muhammad was a man of good reputation, with great influence in the city. When he spoke, he fired the hearts of his listeners. He was called the One Who Can Be Trusted for his fair dealings in business, and he dreamed dreams of the kind lesser men do not.

So the idol-makers trod carefully. "We'll make you King of Mecca if only you will stop your preaching, Muhammad!" they said. "Don't you see how this new religion of yours will damage the trade in idols and cut the revenue of the house of the gods?"

But Muhammad did not care about their greedy profits, and he would not stop preaching what God had told him to preach. "Allah is the one, the only God."

When bribes did not work, the idol-makers used threats. "We'll shun all your tribe and buy nothing from them in the marketplace. Perhaps they can put a stop to this foolishness of yours!"

But Muhammad would not stop his preaching. "Allah is the one, the only God."

Next, the idol-makers pretended to be tolerant. But Muhammad's following was growing. More and more people began to believe what he was saying. Muhammad knew that the idol-makers would resort to violence soon, to put a stop to him.

Some pilgrims from Medina, several hundred miles away, heard Muhammad preach — "Allah is the one, the only God" — and they delighted in his message. "Come and preach in Medina!" they said. "We want our friends, our families, our neighbors to hear you for themselves. Honor us with your presence! Leave behind Mecca and all those who hate you!"

So Muhammad left Mecca with his wife — left the city where he had grown up, left the house of the gods and the company of his tribe. And he walked out along a new road, into a new chapter of his life's story.

Only in the nick of time did he leave. For assassins were on the streets that same night, with drawn knives and murder in their hearts. "Gone? Left to spread his lies further afield? He must be stopped!" The idol-makers were filled with bitter malice and went after Muhammad, armed and on horseback, pursuing a pair of helpless travelers.

The ground shook to the gallop of hooves. When Muhammad looked around, the sun shone on naked swords and spear points. There was only one road, and the idol-makers intended to ride it till they rode down Muhammad and trampled his "message" into the dust.

In a gorge, where the hot sun ricocheted from rock to rock and the air melted and ran, Muhammad sought a hiding place. He found a cave a little way from the track, clambering over rocks and thorns to reach its dark mouth. He and his wife crept inside — it was cool, like a blessing — and crouched down, silent and still, in the rear of the cave.

But the galloping came closer with every second, and now came the noise of voices, too — shouted commands and swords slashing at the brambles. There was not the smallest chance that the cave would escape attention if the pursuers searched the gorge.

The horses came to a halt directly below the cave. Men dismounted, and footsteps could be heard on the grassless ground. There was a rattle of stones as two idol-makers clambered toward the mouth of the cave. Their silhouettes moved across the daylit entrance, and Muhammad's wife huddled closer, pressing her hands over her mouth in terror.

"Look here," said one of the searchers, "a pigeon's nest with a full brood of eggs in it."

The second came to see, but chose not to count the little blue eggs, for it would mean brushing his face against a massive spider's web. The web's geometric threads, strung with dewdrops, shimmered in the sunlight, the tapestried work of weeks by some industrious spider. It clad the cliff face and curtained the cave from portal to portal.

"Well, it's plain no one's been this way for a while," said the men, and turned back down the mountainside.

Muhammad's wife turned to her husband in amazement.

A web? A nest full of unbroken birds' eggs? How had she entered the cave without seeing them? How had they both entered the cave without breaking them? It was impossible, as the idol-makers had rightly thought.

Muhammad was deep in prayer, facing toward the holy city he had left behind. His face was at peace, his praying hands steady, not shaking.

"Of course," thought his wife. Where was her faith that she had feared for their safety? Was not Allah great enough, resourceful enough to protect his own prophet from danger? Was it so incredible that Allah, who made the universe, should have spared the gift of a bird's nest and a spider's web to keep Muhammad and his message alive?

When the idol-makers had gone, Muhammad and his wife continued on their way toward Medina and a new life, breaking free of the past as pigeon chicks break free from their eggs. And eloquent Muhammad went on to weave a web of words that captured the hearts and souls of millions.

Ash

A MAN had four sons, and three of them were his pride and joy. The fourth was his despair. Squat and ugly, he spent all day lolling by the fire, gazing into the flames, never stirring to do a useful day's work. "What are you *doing,* exactly?" his father would ask, losing patience.

"Just thinking." His face was streaked with soot, his clothes grubby with sitting in the warm ashes: his brothers called him Ash. They called him a great many other, less flattering names, as well, and threw things at him — fish bones, apple cores, insults. But Ash hardly noticed. The flames' reflection danced in his bloodshot eyes, and he just went on thinking.

To the whole village, Ash was an idle layabout. They could not pass by without kicking him, could not talk about him without a sneer in their voices and a spit in his direction.

The young women went by giggling and chanting:

"Ash, Ash, go and hunt!
Or is your hunting knife too blunt?
Ash, Ash, make a wish!
Wish you'd ever caught a fish?
Ash, Ash, by the fire,
What made you so awful tired?
Wasn't chasing girls, I bet'ya:
Wouldn't know one if you met her!"

Then one day the neighboring tribe issued a challenge: "Our champion will wrestle yours!"

Ash's brothers, like all the other young men, were thrilled, glad of the excitement, eager to be chosen champion of the tribe . . . until they saw their opponent. Whale Man was as big as a hut and as heavy with blubber as a bull seal. He came through the woods breaking down saplings and knocking bears out of the trees. He picked up a newly carved canoe and threw it like a paper dart, so that it wedged in a mudbank. Then, bellowing like a moose, he kicked a hole in the side of the village longhouse rather than go in through the door.

"Who's it going to be? Whose head shall I rip off today?"

There was a long wait for volunteers.

The village squirmed with shame. The chieftain pondered how many sealskins he must give his neighbors, to make them go away and take their champion with them.

"I'll fight you," said Ash, standing up. "You've put out the fire anyway, with your big feet. So I may as well fight you, to keep warm."

The giant wrestler began to laugh. The women began to laugh with him, to be polite, and then the men joined in, hoping the giant had a sense of humor. Ash? Wrestle?

"You? You couldn't wrestle your way out of a hammock!" hissed his brothers. "Keep quiet; you'll make things worse!"

But Ash simply ducked out through the hole in the wall, waited for Whale Man to follow, and then took hold of him by both feet. Ash shook Whale Man like a blanket till the fleas flew out of his hair, then beat him like a drum till the stains flew off his loincloth. Ash whirled him about by his ears, and flung him into the next valley where he landed with a noise like rotten fruit. When the chief looked around, the challengers were nowhere to be seen.

"How?" he exclaimed.

"Fluke," said one brother.

"Lucky accident," said another.

"Trick of the light," said the third.

But Ash had gone back indoors, anyway, and stretched himself out beside the newly built fire. No one mentioned the matter of the giant again, and he never reminded them.

There was magic in Ash. He must have read it in the embers, or dreamed it in a dream. But somehow there was magic in Ash, and his fellow men chose to ignore it. Magic does not like to be ignored.

Early one morning, a woman emerged from the longhouse, on her way to fetch water. She looked at the skyline and gave a shriek. For lumbering toward her, larger than any giant, were all the trees of the distant forests — on the warpath.

From every side came trees, roots clawing up the soil, knotting their branches into fists, their heads tossing with indignation. "We're surrounded! We're done for!" cried the villagers, clinging to one another. "They'll trample us into the ground!"

Not until the trees were shoulder to shoulder, their branches interlocking, their trunks as close as the bars of a cage, did Ash stir from beside the fire. He stepped to the door of the hut, peered blearily against the bright light, and shouted: "Stop it! Go back! There's no harm done! My word on it!"

The trees faltered and came to a halt. Their dark green tops bent over Ash, like parents bending anxiously over an injured child. Fir cones fell by the hundred on the longhouse roof. Then the trees spun around on their roots and trudged away. With the wind sighing through their green

needles, they sounded like grumpy whisperers.

"That was a narrow escape," said Ash's father.

"Near thing," said his brother.

"Did you hear Ash?" said a second. "Who did he think he was shouting at? Does he really think he made the trees go?"

"Must be even madder than we thought," said the third.

The ground rumbled and the sky shook. The villagers, dawdling back to their work, looked up and saw — no, it could not be — the smallest of changes in the familiar view. The horizon did not seem quite the same shape, the mountains not quite as they had been before.

But the ground rumbled and the sky continued to shake. By noon, they realized the dreadful truth — that the far-off mountains were no longer far away. They had picked up their skirts of grass, flexed their bones of rock, and were moving, purple-headed with anger, across the coastal plain. Where their shoulders rubbed together, sparks flew, and from their clenched fists, boulders tumbled in avalanches of rage.

You see, there was magic in Ash, and magic does not like to be ignored.

Larger and larger loomed the mountains, closing in on every side, while the villagers ran this way and that, but found no escape.

"Ash! Ash! Come out and speak to them! Tell them to stop! Ask them not to crush us! Help us, do!" they begged, but Ash only lazed beside the fire, watching the magic of the flames as usual. At last he got to his feet, went outside, and held up both hands. "Peace. Stand still. That's far enough."

Obedient as dogs, the mountains lay down where they were, jostling, settling, lounging along the ground, the evening sun on their watching faces. This time, when Ash lay back down in his favorite place, the girls brought him food, his brothers brought him drink, and his father threw more wood on the fire.

Now they saw the magic in Ash. His family and tribe stopped calling him a layabout and a fool. Suddenly they were as proud to have him in their midst as any champion wrestler or holy man, and spoke of him boastfully: "We have a man full of magic! The trees and mountains do as he tells them! We have a man who can think all day, without tiring! If only we had his wisdom. If only we had his magic in us!"

One day, visitors came calling. Six men got out of a fine carved canoe and walked up to the village.

"Greetings. Have you come to buy sealskins?" said the villagers, but the strangers answered not a word.

"Have you come in peace? Or to challenge us to wrestle?" said the villagers, but the strangers answered not a word.

"Have you come looking for brides? Or warriors? Or craftsmen? Or fishermen?"

But the strangers simply walked straight ahead into the longhouse and up to the fire where Ash lay thinking.

"I have been expecting you," said Ash, looking up at once. Instead of flames dancing in his eyes, they had become strangely blue, the color of water. "Is your master ill?"

"He is, young man, and if we do not hurry, he may die before we get back to him. Please come."

Ash got up and strode down to the canoe with them. He climbed aboard and took up a paddle, and his powerful arms helped speed the boat out to sea.

Not far from the horizon, where the setting sun gouged a blood-red whirlpool in the sea, the canoe spun around three times, and sank out of sight.

Standing on tiptoe on the shore, the young women wept, and Ash's father wrung his hands. "Death has sent an escort for him! Death has taken away our magical young man!"

But the six messengers were not from Death. They came from the sea caves beneath the setting sun, sent by the strongest man of all. When the canoe touched bottom, all seven got out and began to walk. Stingrays swam by like blankets on a high wind. Dogfish cruised the canyons of weed-hung rock. The sunlight filtered, in a frail dapple, through the choppy surface of the sea, lighting a silver storm of salmon. Across the sea floor, the six messengers led Ash to a deep sea trench. And there, on a bed of sea grass, lay a man so old that his body was more spirit than flesh. It seemed that some monstrous torturer had skewered him to the bed of the sea, for a huge pole stood on his chest, soaring high, high out of view.

"Ah! You have come at last! At last I may rest. At last!" sighed the frail old man, lifting his head a little. "For a thousand years I have held up the sky with this pole. For a thousand years, my strength has been equal to the task. But now I am old and dying, and there is no one but you with magic enough in your soul and strength enough in your breast to balance this pole in my place."

Ash at once lay down beside the old man and took the end of the pole, resting it on his own chest. The soot that had always stained his face had washed clean away. The smuts that had always dirtied his clothes floated away on the tide.

"I am asking much of you, Spotless One," said the weary old man. "What will you do, as the years wash the rocks into sand? What will you do to pass the time away?"

"Oh, that will be no hardship to me," Spotless One replied. "I do not know the meaning of boredom. I shall simply lie here and watch the magic of sunlight dancing on the wave tops. And that will help me think."

The Tower of Babel

A HEBREW MYTH

EARLY IN THE MORNING of the world, before the human race had grown very large at all, it moved all together, one great tribe of wandering nomads pitching their tents where dusk overtook them.

Then one day, in one year, they decided to exchange tents for houses of stone, and they built a city in the center of a great plain, and stopped their wandering. When the city was built, they were very proud of it — overly proud of it, for its gateways and market squares, its staircases and turrets convinced them, "There's nothing we can't do! Let's build a tower as high as Heaven itself, so that people half a world away will see it and wonder!" So they baked bricks and they mixed mortar and they built up . . . and up and up.

When God saw their tower growing, and their pride growing along

51

with the tower, he did not like the idea of the people of Babel reaching so far upward. So he stamped once, and the ground trembled. He breathed once, and the mortar dried to dust and bled from between the bricks. He took one brick from the base of the Tower of Babel, and it fell. Like Satan falling on his belly in the dust, the Tower of Babel tumbled, and with it the pride and ambition of its builders. Clutching each other, clutching at beams of wood and lintels of stone, they plummeted to the ground, rolling and bowling in every direction across the great plain.

And when they opened their mouths to bemoan the disaster, strange words came from between their lips, strange accents and dialects. Tugging at one another's coats, gesticulating with frantic hands, they yelled in each other's faces. But not one man could make sense of what his neighbor said to him; not one woman could make the woman beside her understand.

The great city was never finished. The Tower of Babel was never rebuilt. For with human beings split and divided by differences of language, they found it very hard to work, or even to think, in harmony.

They have never learned the trick of it, not even in all these years.

Saint Christopher

A EUROPEAN LEGEND

CHRISTOPHER was born neither good nor bad, but he knew his worth. "I'm strong, I'm tall, I can turn my hand to most things. I shall work for only the best. I shall take for my master the most powerful ruler in the world." So he went down to Hell to serve the Devil, because he had heard that more people feared the Devil than any other emperor or tyrant. Certainly the Devil's banners were to be seen flying everywhere on earth.

At the door of Hell, there was a long line of people wanting to sign up in the Devil's service. At last Christopher and one other man were admitted into the presence of the Lord of Darkness, who sat on a throne of fire, eating sparks.

"Swear to obey me in all things," said the Devil (which was the way of masters and servants in those days).

"What should I swear by?" asked the other applicant. "By my mother? On my life? By Jesus Christ?"

At the mention of Christ's name, the Devil gave a shudder, and his red eyes rolled. Christopher had sudden misgivings. Quickly, he made the sign of the cross — he had often seen Christians do it — touching his forehead, chest, then each shoulder. Sure enough, the Devil leaped out of his chair and ran. "Don't do that! Don't! If you're going to work for me, don't ever do that, d'you hear?"

"Work for him?" thought Christopher, as the Devil slammed the chamber door. "I set out to work for the most powerful master in the world. Plainly this Jesus Christ is more powerful."

So he made it his business to find out all about Jesus. And he liked what he heard.

"What must I do to serve this Jesus Christ?" he asked a priest.

"Serve your fellow men. Either by prayer, as a monk, or by making yourself useful to those in need."

"You mean I don't get to meet him? Not meet my own master?"

"Not in this life, Christopher. In this life you will only see Christ's face in the faces of the poor and needy."

Now Christopher was not of a nature suited to a monk's life, so he decided to make himself useful in some practical way. He built himself a hut beside a river, and whenever travelers needed to cross over, he carried them across the river on his strong shoulders. Whole families of eight and nine children he could carry, though the current was strong and the river cold and wide. As he carried them, he would listen to their sad stories, and make the children laugh and the adults brighten, while he sang a song or told a fable.

One day, a little boy came to the river. "I want to cross over," he said.

Christopher swung him onto his shoulders as a swimmer might hang a towel around his neck, and broke into a cheerful song.

But a short way out from the shore, he had to stop singing. The boy was much heavier than he looked. "I must be getting old," Christopher told his passenger. "I've carried ten of your size before now, without thinking twice!"

Halfway across the river, the child began to feel even heavier. Christopher could hardly lift his head or straighten his back. "What age did you say you were, boy?" But the boy did not reply.

With every step, the boy grew heavier, so that soon Christopher could barely keep his footing. The river shoved at him, and the weight on his back bore down like a bale of wool, a full barrel, a hod of bricks. He staggered and gasped for breath. His mouth was being pushed under, his nose too. He had either to let go of the boy or drown. He turned his face toward the sky and took a last gulp of air. "I fear, son, that I cannot . . ."

And yet he must. How could he let a child drown whom he had offered to carry? He must get the boy to the shore, even if it cost him his last ounce of strength. The river swamped him. The boy's hand, clutched in his hair, seemed to be plucking out his brain, and yet he plunged on, his face submerged now, his lungs bursting. In his heart, he prayed: not to live, but that the boy should not drown.

At last, his feet felt shallower ground and he crawled up the bank on all fours and dropped on his face underneath the boy.

"Thank you," said the child, "but I have no money to pay you."

Christopher did not want to frighten him by saying how close they had both come to drowning, so he simply rolled on to his back, smiled through his sodden beard, and said what he always said. "No charge, son. I did it for Christ."

"You speak truer than you know," said the boy in a deep, musical voice, then ran away, fast as a deer, across the wooded landscape.

Christopher lay on his back looking up at the sky. And when he had breath enough to speak what he had realized, he shouted up at the birds: "No wonder he weighed so much! I wasn't carrying a child — I was carrying the greatest man in the world! I met Jesus today, and carried him on my back!"

And that is why travelers pray to Saint Christopher for a safe journey, because everyone needs kindness from those they meet on a journey; a helping hand, a glimpse of Christ's smile on the face of a stranger.

God Moves Away

A MYTH FROM TOGO

"I TELL YOU God lives above the sky. Way up high. Out of earshot almost. We know about these things in Togo."

"Are you saying God never lived on earth, among men?"

"Not at all. Of course he did! The sky hung about here, not much higher than a man's head, and God used it for a hammock. But he moved away. Don't you know that? Don't you know why?"

"I know you're going to tell me."

People were disrespectful, yes. Little children used to wipe their greasy hands on the sky at the end of a meal, and cooks used to tear pieces off, for the cooking pot. I hear it was delicious — gave you wind, but it was delicious.

You know how the women pound corn into meal in this part of the

57

world? With a big wooden bowl to hold the grain, and a huge wooden pestle for pounding it? Bang, bang, bang. Well, naturally the pestle needs to thump down on the corn as hard as possible. So this old lady used to throw the pestle high in the air. It was made from a tree trunk and was as tall as she was, but she could thump that pestle up and down for hours on end, like an elephant stomping on peanuts. And of course every time she threw the pestle upward, it used to give God a hard whack somewhere painful. One day it hit him in the eye.

That made him so mad that he packed up and left. He did! Rolled up the sky and flew right up high, rubbing his eye and muttering.

Of course it was a help to the old woman's work, but a great sadness to everyone else. No more sky in the cooking pot. Nowhere to wipe their greasy hands. And — worst of all — it made a conversation with God so difficult. So hard to make him hear our prayers. So hard to take an argument before him for his judgment.

The old woman did what she could to make amends. She told her children and her grandchildren and every other greasy-handed child in the village to gather up all the pounding bowls.

Some still had corn in them. Some had rainwater slopping about in the bottom. Some were old and bruised with fifty years of pounding. But the old lady piled them all up, one on top of the next, and climbed up, to ask God if he wouldn't come back down where he belonged.

She nearly made it, too. When she reached the top of the pile and was balanced in the topmost bowl, like an egg in an eggcup, she could almost reach the hem of God's robe. She stood on tiptoe. She hopped as high as she dared, but it made the tower wobble alarmingly.

"One more bowl and I'm there!" she called down to her children. But there were no more bowls to be had. "I know!" she called. "Take the bottom one out and pass it up to me. Then I'll be able to reach!"

And that is what they did, for it is a foolish child who argues with his grandmother. They took away the bottom pounding bowl — *wobble, clatter, eeek!* — and though the old lady made a snatch for the hem of God's robe, she missed. And that was that.

Wilhelm Tell

A SWISS LEGEND

"TO LIFE, Liberty, and a free Switzerland!" That was the toast they drank and the oath they swore in secret. But in public, few dared to defy the tyranny of the Austrian Empire. So they paid the heavy taxes, they obeyed the unfair laws, and in secret they dreamed of independence and swore grand oaths to keep from despairing.

Wilhelm Tell was different. A farmer from a remote mountain farm, he spoke little and thought deeply. So when he swore such an oath, the words dropped like hot sealing wax onto a deed of law, and made those who heard him tremble at the strength of his feelings.

In every respect, Tell was the best of men: best archer, best mountaineer, best helmsman at a boat's tiller out on Lake Lucerne, best friend to have when a friend was needed, best father in all the world, as far as his son

Carl was concerned. Many suspected that, since the Austrians had come to power, a temper burned like volcanic lava in Tell's breast, but his friends and family had never seen it flare. It was that family of his that kept Wilhelm at one remove from the politics of rebellion. Only a bachelor can afford reckless exploits in the name of Liberty; a married man has other lives than his own to consider.

One cruelty gave the Austrian overlords a taste for another and another. Men like Baron Gessler delighted in inventing new humiliations to inflict on the Swiss. An edict forbade any farmer the use of a horse or ox to pull his plow. The farmer could haul his own plow, couldn't he, and give the horse and ox to his Austrian betters.

Baron Gessler stalked the streets and lanes, surrounded by bodyguards, to glory in the misery he caused. In fact, power was making Gessler a little peculiar, a little wild in the eye, a little unpredictable in his extravagant malice. He placed various of his hats on poles and sent them into the market square of every village, demanding that everyone who passed by must bow to the hat, as though to its owner. Soldiers were posted at the foot of each pole, to ensure everyone complied with the decree.

Old men with arthritic joints were obliged to bend their aching knees to Gessler's hat. Young women carrying babies, farmers laden with bales of hay were called on to pay their respects to the silly hat on high. Milk-maids could not sell their milk in the marketplace until they had curtseyed to Gessler's hat. From the window of an inn in Altdorf, Gessler himself watched, grinning, and thought of the same scene being acted out all over the canton.

It so happened that Wilhelm Tell chose that day to come to town for supplies. Nothing was farther from his mind than to make trouble: he had brought his dear son Carl with him. But no one had told him about the business of Gessler's hat, and as he crossed the square, one of the soldiers suddenly barked like a rabid dog, "Bow to the hat, why don't you?"

"Why would I bow to a hat?" inquired Tell in his low, shy voice.

"Because it's the hat of Baron Gessler, and it represents him."

Wilhelm squinted up at the hat. "It might bear a passing resemblance to him, I suppose, if he ate less … But the day I bow to a hat is the day I grow ears and bray like a donkey. Bow to it yourself."

With the bang of a door and the breaking of a beer mug, Baron Gessler came bellying out of the inn. A gobbet of chewed apple flew from his mouth as he blared, "So! You refuse to obey my decree, do you? I've heard of you! You're Wilhelm Tell! I know all about you! You're famous hereabouts, aren't you? People never stop talking about you — What a good archer! What a great mountaineer! And you're a dissident, are you? A subversive? A rebel?"

Suddenly guards were clinging to Tell like squirrels to a tree.

"That's a lot to accuse me of, simply because I insulted your hat," said Tell calmly.

"So will you bow to it?"

"No."

Gessler burst into hysterical laughter that puffed out his cheeks and made his forehead red. "Then your farm's forfeit! I'll lock you up! I'll have you sent to Castle Kussnacht and . . ." Tell's gray eyes looked back at him, cold and unmoved. Gessler racked his brains for something more original in the way of cruelty. The longer Tell retained his dignity here in this public square, the more Gessler was the one being made to look small. He peered beyond Tell and saw something that inspired his malicious imagination . . . "Unless . . ."

Tell flexed his arm muscles, which were growing uncomfortable. A guard slithered to the ground. "Unless?" he asked, quietly.

"I hear you've a fair art with a crossbow. What a waste it would be to bury such talent in a dungeon!" Gessler looked down at the remains of the apple he had been eating. "If you can shoot through this apple at a distance of one hundred paces, you can go free."

"Agreed!" said Tell, taken aback by such uncharacteristically good sportsmanship.

Gessler hiccuped with laughter. "Guards. Balance this apple on the head of Tell's son, and stand him in front of that tree yonder. That should help make Herr Wilhelm shoot straight!"

Up until that moment, Tell had been so intent on keeping his temper that he had forgotten entirely about Carl, about his little boy standing so still and wide-eyed in his father's long shadow. For the first time Gessler saw the flicker of fear he so loved to inflict. Tell was afraid to make the shot. He would crumble now, in front of all his admiring neighbors, and beg for mercy.

Nobody moved for a long time. Nobody moved until Carl reached out, took the half-eaten apple out of Gessler's hand, and set off toward the tree. Along the shore of the lake he walked. One hundred paces? It was more like one hundred and fifty. Carl rested his back against the trunk and looked back at his father, so small now in the distance. "You can do it, Father!" he called. His high, sweet voice rang out as clear as a bell.

The soldiers tied Carl to the tree with ropes. They made as if to blindfold him, too. "I won't flinch, if that's what you think," he told them. "I know my father can hit the apple."

So he saw the huge crowd that had gathered seemingly from nowhere. He saw his father's face above the level crossbow — pale as snow on the mountaintops. He saw the sun flaring on the water of the lake, a blinding brightness. He saw the metal bolt glint in the sun, the flash of a second one held between his father's fingers. Carl held his breath. A cloud covered the sun.

The bolt flew so fast that the twang of the bowstring and thud of the impact were like a single sound. A woman in the crowd screamed, *"You murderer, Gessler!"*, for she had seen, through her fingers, an explosion of white and red as the bolt struck.

But it was only the apple splattering to pulpy pieces. Fragments stuck to the boy's hair, juice trickled into his eyes, as he smiled back at his father. Then a cheer went up from the Swiss crowd that was repeated at every window, shouted down every alleyway in Altdorf: *"He did it! Tell hit the apple!"*

Gessler, blustering and foolish, groped for something disparaging to say. "Not so cocky, really, were you, Tell? Thought it might take two shots?" He pointed out the second bolt between Tell's fingers.

The archer shrugged. "Oh yes, I thought my first bolt might kill my son. That's why I had a second ready for you, Gessler."

"Arrest him! Seize him! Traitor! Villain! Assassin!" Gessler ducked behind a member of his bodyguard, his heart leaping with a mixture of terror and triumph, a cold sweat running down his fat neck. "Your own words condemn you! Take him to Castle Kussnacht and let him wait in a dungeon for the headman's axe!"

A murmur like a hive of bees stirred among the crowd. Then an egg hit the back of Gessler's coat, a hail of pebbles began to fly. If Gessler had wanted to upset the people of Altdorf, he had surely succeeded, for they began to herd forward, like cattle roused by lightning.

"Run, Carl! Run!" cried Tell, and Carl picked up his heels and ran into the shelter of the crowd, which swallowed him up, hiding him as surely as if he were invisible.

Arrest Tell? When he had won his freedom like that? Some injustices can be borne, some wickednesses tolerated. But this time Gessler had touched a nerve already rubbed raw by his tyranny. Someone smashed a market stall and began handing out sticks of wood for weapons. Some drew the money from their pockets — worthless Austrian coppers good for nothing but pelting worthless Austrians.

"It's no good, sir. We'll never reach the horses!" shouted the captain of the guard. "Best get offshore. That's our only hope." And so they beat an undignified retreat, jogging along a jetty, bundling Tell aboard a small fishing boat. The crowd also broke into a run, shaking their sticks and shouting, "Get Gessler! Let's put a stop to him once and for all!"

"Steer, won't you?" Gessler pushed a sergeant in the chest.

"B-but I don't know how to —"

"Just do it, fool, before this rabble tears us limb from limb!"

As the space widened between boat and shore, Gessler crowed like a cock. "Just wait till my *real* troops arrive!" he sneered at the people ranged along the jetty. *"You'll wish you'd never been born!"*

A sudden yaw in the boat made him stagger, and he cursed the helmsman. Then he saw the cause: a storm like a genie summoned from a bottle. Lake Lucerne, too, was rising up against tyranny and injustice.

There were blades of cold and arrows of ice in the wind. They sheered through the rigging and brought down the topsails onto the men below. The unwilling helmsman cowered in the bottom of the boat, pleading for the help of a real sailor. "Free Tell! He knows boats. He can sail anything! Free Tell or *we'll all drown!*"

"So even you admire the lout!" fumed Gessler. His opulent, fur-lined coat was so heavy with rain and spray that his knees were bowing. "All right. All right! Cut the dog loose."

The moment his hands were untied, Tell took the tiller of the boat and turned her into the wind. She stopped rolling and pitching and taking in water, and beyond that no one cared where she was heading. Minutes later, they saw the shore dead ahead, spines of jagged rock clawing the waves into an open wound of breaking water, a foaming maelstrom. They

stared openmouthed, letting the driving rain trickle down their throats. Did Tell mean to wreck the boat and take his enemies with him to the bottom of the lake?

At the last second, Tell swung on the tiller, and every man aboard was sent sprawling. The prow reared up like a horse's head, the keel grazed bottom. The boat swung around within its own length, so that it was stern-on to the rocks. And from the stern transom leaped Wilhelm Tell — out across a gulf of rioting water, black, deep and deadly. It was a phenomenal leap — a mountain goat's leap from one crag to the next. Only a mountaineer could have made it and held his balance on landing. Only the bravest could have made it in the teeth of a gale, while the wavetops gnashed and the foam flew like blinding snow. Only Wilhelm Tell could have done it with an iron crossbow slung across his back, snatched from the slippery deck the moment before he jumped.

The Austrian guards clung desperately to the boat rail, unwilling to let go despite Gessler's ranting: *"Shoot him! Shoot the villain! Kill him! Don't let him get away, Devil curse you!"*

The boat had the wind behind it now, and was driven out toward the center of the lake, ropes snaking, sail ripping, and the tiller unmanned. On the shore, clambering agilely over the razor-sharp rocks, a figure lithe as an otter reached the safety of dry land.

"I'll see you in hell for this!" bawled Gessler. "You so-called soldiers! You and your wives and sweethearts! I'll finish Tell! I'll burn down his farm with his wife and brat inside! I'll burn down every farm on the mountain! I'll burn down Altdorf!" The wind dropped suddenly, as if outbrayed by Gessler's cursing. The rain teemed blackly, but the drifting boat ceased her pitching as the storm stood still in horror.

The figure on the shore laid a single bolt to his crossbow and took aim. Despite a furlong of darkness crammed with rain between him and the boat, and all his breath used up, Tell fired. And the insane ranting on the boat stopped even more suddenly than the wind's howl had done.

Next morning found the boat adrift in the heart of Lake Lucerne. The soldiers aboard, when asked what had become of the Baron, only pointed over the side at the still, secretive waters. Lake Lucerne is deep. It takes time to give up its captives. But the fishermen of the lake said that a great many fish died that night, as if poisoned by some pollution of the water.

The Swiss will only stand for just so much. They may bend to circumstance. They may bear with misfortune. But ultimately, they are slaves to no one. Within half a handful of years, Switzerland was free of Austria. It has never given up its independence since.

A Heart of Stone

A GREEK MYTH

"LOVE," said the King, "has never troubled me, I'm glad to say." In fact, King Pygmalion of Cyprus had done rather better than simply not falling in love. He had managed to loathe women, with a deep and deadly loathing, ever since he had been able to tell them apart from men. "Can't see the purpose of them," he would say, in a superior way. "Don't hunt elephants. Don't quarry rocks . . ."

If these seem strange virtues to set any great store by, it should be explained that Pygmalion was a sculptor as well as a king. His notion of true joy was a tusk of ivory or a block of marble, uncut, awaiting the touch of his chisel. He carved animals, heroes, children, pillars . . . and superbly, too. People could almost forgive him his hatred of women when they saw the genius of his carvings.

70

Venus did not forgive so easily. The Goddess of Love took great exception to his rude and ignorant remarks. Every day, from the slopes of Mount Olympus where the gods of Greece made their home, she could hear the supercilious voice of Pygmalion complaining: how women *talked*, how women *lied*, how women *spent money*, how women were a useless and troublesome invention he could well do without. Not surprisingly, he had never offered up a single sacrifice in the Temple of Venus. One day Venus stamped her foot, and her green eyes flashed with resolve. "It is time, Pygmalion, to teach you a lesson!"

A stranger knocked at the door of Pygmalion's workroom next day — a tall hooded stranger with piercing green eyes.

"Greetings, your majesty. I am a traveler returned from foreign parts, where I learned of a contest that might interest you. The King of Crete is offering a laurel wreath for the finest sculpture submitted. I thought of you at once, O King, knowing you to be the finest sculptor in the world."

"Thank you! I shall carve a bull!" exclaimed Pygmalion, already selecting the ideal block from among the marble stacked in the yard. "The Cretans like nothing better than a charging . . ."

"No, no!" interrupted the stranger. "The statue must be of a woman. The one considered the most beautiful will be the winner."

"Oh, but I never . . ."

But when Pygmalion turned round, there was no one to be seen.

Overcoming his disgust, Pygmalion decided to compete nevertheless, and to carve a female figure. He chose the finest marble, sharpened his best tools, and asked himself what could possibly make a *woman* seem beautiful. "A wide, generous mouth," he thought, "but not always talking. A pair of large, tender eyes looking only at me. Hair flowing like the weed in a river, fit to drown a man . . ."

The figure that emerged from under his skillful fingers was tall and willowy, bending a little forward. She seemed to be listening with intent interest to everything Pygmalion had to say. "I think you will do very nicely," he found himself saying aloud to the sweetly inclined head, as he set down his tools. "For a woman, you are really quite . . . quite . . . exquisite, if I do say so myself." But the statue only looked back at him, with white marble eyes and a sweet but brittle smile.

When the King went to bed that night, he could not get the statue out of his mind. It was his best achievement yet, no doubt about it. It was perfect. He had to get up and go back to the workroom just to look at it, at her. For the rest of the night he sat there, gazing at her, enthralled by the beauty of his own making.

Next morning he found himself unwilling to crate up his statue and dispatch her to Crete. No sooner were the nails banged home than he pried them out again and recovered his masterpiece from the crate, setting her on a plinth where the sunlight flattered her lovely figure, her delicate features, her long curling hair. "I shall call you Galatea," he said, but her carved mouth did not respond, either to agree or disagree. She seemed more beautiful every time he looked at her, but cold and still. She seemed on the very point of moving — and yet she would never move. She was only a statue, after all.

For a week, Pygmalion did not leave his workroom. His servants brought meat and drink to the door, but he sent them away. His ministers could get no answer to their knocking. They gathered around the door, anxious, worried. Then, when he did finally emerge, he rushed past them, white-faced, and ran all the way to the Temple of Venus on the hill, falling on his knees in front of the altar.

"O Goddess of Love, take pity on me! I'm a fool, I know it! I'm half-mad, I see that! But I can't help myself! I love her! I've fallen in love with my own statue! I deserve to be laughed at in the street — 'There goes that fool who lost his heart to a piece of marble!' — but I never knew what it was like before. I never even guessed love could be like this! Pity me, goddess! Take this pain from my heart, this madness out of my brain! I'll carve your statue at every crossroads — if only you'll end this *pain!*"

His voice rang around the cavernous temple. The only faces looking down at him were images of the goddess Venus — tall, enthroned in a sea shell, clothed in locks of hair, carved in pallid stone.

He walked back to the workroom, scuffing the heels of his sandals. He might have gone to his palace, but the statue drew him, as a magnet draws iron. He must see it again, even though seeing it only increased his suffering, because it could never be anything but cold, insensible marble.

The look on his face was so terrible that his ministers and servants stepped back and did not try to speak to him. Pygmalion closed the door behind him and leaned against it, his eyes tight shut in self-loathing. "Oh, what I'd give to be one of those lucky men I used to make fun of — in love with some dancer or priestess or orange-seller!"

"Are you speaking to me?"

He opened his eyes and saw at once that his statue was missing, his beloved statue. *"Where is she? What have you done with my statue?"* The stranger sitting in the seat by the window was so blotted out by the sunlight behind her that he saw only a dark shadow. But when she stood up — "I'm sorry, what statue?" — he could see her more clearly: a beauty in green drapery and gold sandals, her hair falling in ringlets to the front and back of her shoulders.

"I believe I may be a little unwell," she said, in a sweet apologetic voice, "for I cannot entirely remember how I came to be here. My name is . . ."

"Galatea," said Pygmalion at once.

"That's right. How did you know? Or are we acquainted? You do seem rather familiar . . . if only I could remember. But I mustn't keep you from your work. I see you are a very fine sculptor, and I know how artists need peace and quiet."

Thus Venus gave Pygmalion his perfect woman, satisfied that he had learned his lesson. Besides, she was extremely eager to see those statues he had promised to carve of her standing at every crossroads.

If the gods have one weakness, it is probably their vanity.

Babushka

A RUSSIAN LEGEND

THE STAR shone — but then everything in Babushka's house shone, bright and glistening. So that when she glimpsed the new star shining in at the corner of the window, she saw nothing unusual in that. Everyone else in the village was out of doors, pointing and prattling. But Babushka would never waste her time so frivolously. She had a house to keep clean, washing and washing-up to do, weeding and baking. She was too busy for wonders.

"A new star! See?"

"Never there before!"

"Last night it was over yonder."

"It's moving!"

"Shifting!"

"Shining!"

"Amazing!"

"Wonderful!"

But Babushka was too busy for wonders.

She heard the new commotion in the street, too, the children oohing and aahing, the *harrumph* of camels and the jingling of bridle bells.

"See their turbans!"

"See their cloaks!"

"See the scrolls and scriptures in their saddlebags!"

But nothing could make Babushka break off from her work until that knock at the door.

"May we rest here tonight, Babushka?" Three travelers stood in her neat little garden; their camels were tethered by the gate. Their clothes were dirty with the dust of many miles, but not so dusty that she could not see the quality and richness of their foreign weave.

"You'd best come in, sirs," said Babushka in a shy whisper, "though if you'd wipe your feet on the mat I'd be grateful."

She bustled about fetching them cheese and milk, dates and nuts, bread and little cakes.

"Sit down and talk to us, Babushka," said her visitors, but Babushka never sat down. There was far too much to do — especially with visitors in the house. There were blankets to be fetched for their beds, fires to be lit, apples to be polished for their dessert.

After dinner, the three foreign gentlemen, Caspar, Melchior, and Balthazar, opened out maps on the table and discussed where their journey was taking them. "We are following the new star," they explained, when she brought them extra candles. "It's leading us to the realm of a new king."

"A new king. Fancy!" said Babushka, but she was too busy washing up the supper things to say more.

"The Christ of the Scriptures!" said Caspar. "The Savior of the World! The star marks his coming — writing it in the sky!"

"The Savior of the World? Well, God bless us!" said Babushka.

"We're taking him presents," said Melchior. "Gold and spices and rich ointments."

"Fortunate man," said Babushka.

"No, no! Only a baby as yet," Balthazar corrected her. "A newborn king!"

'Then may he live long, for his mother's sake," said Babushka, and the three turned quickly and looked at her, simply because at last she had stopped stock-still. She stood by the door, her shawl clutched close at her throat. "I had a child once," she said, "but he died." Then, seeing the pity in their faces, she put on a bright smile and set off once more, straightening the ornaments, plumping the cushions, sweeping crumbs from under the table. "No great matter. I keep busy. Children! They make a house untidy anyway."

"Come with us, Babushka," said Caspar.

"Come where, sir?"

"Yes, come with us tomorrow," said Melchior. "What's to stop you?"

"Come and see the Savior?" said Babushka. "You shouldn't tease an old woman."

"Why not come?" said Balthazar. "You've nothing to keep you here."

Babushka put her hands on her hips and laughed, though she had not laughed for many years. "Lord bless you, there's a man talking! Nothing to keep me? Why, there's the washing and the wiping, the sweeping and the shopping, the dusting and the dishes. A person can't just get up and go on the spur of the moment — not someone like me, I mean! It's one thing for you sages and scholars, you thinkers and philosophers!" But she would have liked to go! Indeed she would! Her gray eyes shone as they had not done for many years. "Besides, I have no present to give the Savior."

In the morning, the three sages said to her again, "Come with us, Babushka! Come and see the Christ child."

"Maybe," she said, giving them parcels of food for the journey. "Soon, perhaps. Maybe I'll follow on tomorrow and catch you up."

"Don't leave it too late," warned Melchior, as he mounted his kneeling camel.

So the three sages went on their way, and the bells on the camels' bridles jingled more and more softly as they swayed away into the distance.

Babushka cleaned her house from top to bottom. "I will go!" she resolved. She washed her clothes for the journey. She mended and polished her boots. "I do have a present, after all!"

She unlocked the cupboard in the corner of the room and took out the toys that had belonged to her dead child. Then she cleaned and painted and polished and mended them all: wooden dolls and little cups, a ball, a bat, a bear. She worked all day and never noticed how the time sped by, for she liked to be busy. For a time she wept at the memory of her dead child. Then she smiled at the thought of the child newly born. How good it would be to welcome such a child into the world! How fine that the three sages thought that she — Babushka! — was a fit person to meet the Savior of the World.

At last she packed all the toys into a basket, shut the door of her immaculate little cottage, and set off after Caspar, Melchior, and Balthazar. The new star in the sky had set, but it was not difficult to follow the trail of excitement and astonishment left behind by the exotic camel train.

She followed them down valleys and over hills, through villages and cities. She followed them to Jerusalem, where they had visited the palace of the Roman Governor. She followed them to Bethlehem, and rested there at an inn.

"Three wise men from foreign parts?" said the innkeeper. "Yes, they came here, but they've gone now. So have the man and woman — and the baby, too."

"The baby was born here?" asked Babushka in amazement.

"Yes, yes. In the stable. No room here. What a night we had! Visitors, lights, singing . . . Gone now, though. You're too late."

Into Egypt, Babushka followed the rumors of Mary and Joseph and their little baby, Jesus. North, west, east and south, she went on searching for the Christ child. Though her search led her nowhere, and lasted many years, she never gave up. On and on she carried her basket of toys, forgetting that the baby king must have long since grown to manhood.

Thirty years later, passing again one day by the walls of Jerusalem, she saw a terrible sight. Three men had been executed by the Romans, nailed by their hands and feet to wooden crosses on a bare hilltop, to suffer in the sun and to die. The one in the center wore a crude twist of thorns around his head, like an imitation crown. A crowd of women stood nearby, weeping. One was the mother of the young man in the crown of thorns.

Babushka set down her heavy basket, and put her arms around the woman. "I lost a son, too," she said. "My heart goes out to you." Then she stooped to pick up her basket again.

It seemed strangely light — as if all the toys had been taken from inside. But no, when she opened the lid, they were still there, as shining and pretty as the day she packed them.

Babushka continued on her way, searching, always searching. But now she decided not to save all the toys in her basket to present to the Christ child. She would give some of them away — "After all, every child is a child of God!" She felt sure the Christ child would understand, when at last she found him. So whenever she passed the home of a child, she left a little something by the hearth — a trumpet, a puppet, a drum.

Strange to say, her basket — though it was now as light as a feather — never emptied. Whenever she reached her hand under the lid, there was still always a variety of toys at her fingertips.

She never did find whom she was looking for — and never realized that she had found him already. She is traveling still, still giving away her toys. She leaves her presents in every Christian country, in every Christian town, on every day of the year. But only on the birthday of the Christ child are her shining gifts visible to the girls and boys who wake in the half-light of morning and remember, "It's Christmas Day!"

The Pig Goes Courting

A HAWAIIAN MYTH

HE WAS NOT a pretty lad. Even his mother and father blanched at their first sight of him: it was the way his snout snuffled and his ears drooped and his tusks curled right back over his ears. His manners left something to be desired, too: the way he held his bowl to his face and grunted down his food, then rooted about the floor for what he had spilled. But when it came to friendship, Kamapua'a was the man to have by you, and when it came to valor, he made the finest ally in the world. The fact that Kamapua'a had the head and body of a pig was of no importance to those who knew him. And he was a god, after all.

He lived on the island of Hawaii, where he spent most of his time frightening away invaders. There was not a foe born who did not panic and run at the sight of Kamapua'a in full charge — head down, shoulders up, tusks gleaming, and venting the most terrifying squeals. He wielded a palm tree for a club, and while he rooted about for coconuts to pitch at retreating enemies, he would scoop up huge earthworks and sand dunes, the better to defend the islanders.

Sometimes, however, when Kamapua'a's mind turned from war to the finer things of life, he would trot off on his human feet, into the hills and plantations, and whistle at the pretty women swaying by. The women would laugh and cast a flirting glance, then patter home to their mothers, giggling. One day, Kamapua'a ventured further inland — to the mountainous regions — and saw a quite different breed of woman. She took away too much of his breath for him to whistle. "Her I shall marry," declared the pig god, gazing up at the summit where Pele stood, red hair streaming.

Pele was the fire goddess. She lived among her cantankerous relations, the volcanoes, whose grumbling could be heard all over the island. Like them, Pele had a fiery disposition (as you might expect of a fire goddess). She greeted Kamapua'a's proposal of marriage with a cackle of crackling laughter, and kicked pebbles down on his head. Then, standing on the skyline, her hands on her hips, she began to heap such invective on the pig god that his little legs bowed.

"Marry you? *You?* The nut-snuffling, trough-grubbing, bristle-backed hog of a bacon-flitch? You sugarcane-crashing bore? You yard of lard? Who do you think you're speaking to?"

"I'm a boar, not a bore," said Kamapua'a, grinning with delight, "and who else in the world do you think is going to take you, you lump of hot coal, you furnace-mouth, you spark-burned hearthrug?"

Pele thumbed her nose. "Filthy mud-rolling, rubbish-eating, snout-nosed heap of brawn!"

"You collision of glowworms! Bad-dream-on-a-hot-night! Indigestible bunch of red chilies!"

Pele spat fire, but Kamapua'a simply raised up a mound of earth to deflect it. "Come down and take the only bridegroom who'll ever have you! Together we'll be pork and crackling!"

So they went on, hurling insults as big as coconuts, until their relations

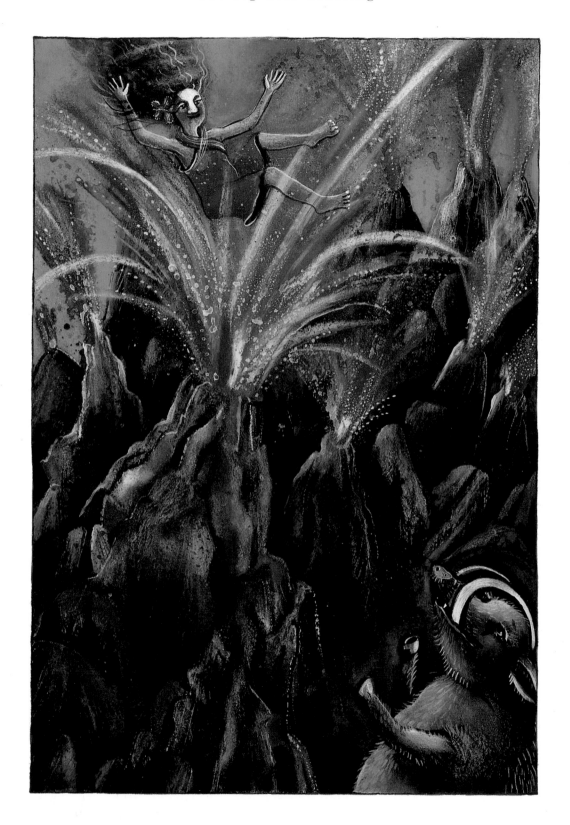

began to join in. The volcanoes trembled, and their vents poured out foul-smelling jets of yellow sulfur. Lightning jumped about excitedly, jabbing a stabbing finger at Kamapua'a and his family and using such words as burned holes in the heavens. Kamapua'a's friends rallied to him in defence of his good name.

It began to look less like a wooing than a war, as the two sides bombarded each other with aspersions and expletives. Words gave way to weapons. At first, Pele only hurled thunderbolts and fireballs, while Kamapua'a threw back cakes of mud and litter off the beach: seaweed and empty turtle shells. But the squabbling escalated.

"Go home, you ugly brute, or my aunts and uncles will erupt and drown you all in molten lava!"

"Look out, Kamapua'a," muttered his friends uneasily. "They could do us in if they put their minds to it."

"Not if we call up reinforcements," said Kamapua'a, scratching himself luxuriously against a palm tree. He turned his snout toward the sky and bellowed: *"Come clouds! Come sparkling springs, come damp dewfall and splashy sea! Come wet rain and fuming fog! Come moist mists and running rivers! Rise up and teach these volcanoes a lesson that will silence their grumbling forever! I'll have you pleading to marry me, Pele, you see if I don't!"*

So all the moist things of the islands ganged together. Springwater leaped up and, together with streams and rills and rivers, ringed the mountains around with water. But when the cascades of orange lava spilled from the throats of Pele's ghastly relations, they dissolved the water in clouds of steam. Mountains of ash blotted out the sky and rained down, hot and choking, on the pig god, till he stood hock-deep in cinders. But he simply blared at the clouds to do their worst, and the clouds burst over the volcanoes and drenched them in torrents of rain.

Magma seethed and bubbled. Brimstone and pumice rattled down on Kamapua'a, white-hot or dripping orange lava. But though he squealed earsplitting yelps of rage, he also summoned up the fogs and mists that live in the morning forests. Like gigantic ghosts, they advanced on the erupting uplands, grappling and interweaving with the yellow clouds of sulfurous smoke, the plumes of steam. There was a hissing like a million angry snakes, a coughing and choking, a spluttering and sputtering. Then, one by one, like snuffed candles, the volcanic fires went out, and Pele's aunts and uncles were reduced to rumbling grumblers, chuntering and mumbling: "... These disrespectful youngsters ..."

Pele, her red hair hanging in sodden hanks, came stumbling blindly through the dense fog, feeling her way and shivering. Kamapua'a plunged forward and, before her eyes even opened, took Pele's two hands in his. "Give in to me, Lady of Fire! The world is more water than fire; my longing for you will always be greater than your loathing. Give in. Fire and earth and air and water should work together — make something out of nothing — not reduce the world to dust and ashes! Let's join forces, you and I. I may look more pig than man, but you'll find I'm more god than either."

She never made a quiet bedfellow. Pele's temper was forever flaring up. But her passion for Kamapua'a, once lit, was as hot as her temper. And soon, when her uncles and aunts grumbled and rumbled at the heart of the island, complaining that the world was changing, Pele would laugh as loud as Kamapua'a, and they would run down to the beach together and drink coconut milk till both their snouts were quite white.

Can Krishna Die?

AN INDIAN LEGEND

MANY GODS have visited the earth. Wherever their feet trod, myths have grown up, and wherever they lived, legends are left, like fossils, in the rocks. But none of the gods has stayed long. For gods can only visit by becoming flesh and blood, and flesh and blood are vulnerable, like butter in the hot sun.

When the great Lord Krishna was born to live among the cowherds and milkmaids of Yadava, however, it seemed he must live forever. He was so strong that no man or beast or monster could overpower him. He was such a warrior that no enemy could stand in his way. He was so handsome that women cherished him as a child and adored him as a grown man. He had children, and his children had children, and it seemed that Krishna must live to bless and protect his family through endless generations. Old age ran off him like rain off a raven's wing.

Then, one day, a joke went badly wrong. A band of wise men came wandering through the meadows, frail, gaunt, aged, and without one smile between them. The young cowherds of Yadava had no respect for their age and wisdom.

"Let's see if they're really so wise," said one.

"Let's see if they even know a cow from a bull!" said another.

They called Samba, grandson of Krishna, and dressed him in women's clothes. His long hair was curly and his cheek was smooth, so that once dressed in a sari, he looked as pretty as any milkmaid. In his right hand he held a pestle for pounding rice, under his dress a cushion, and on his face a silly simper.

"O wise men! O sage scholars of a thousand learned words! Cast your clever eyes over this girl and tell us what manner of child she will have when it is born."

Samba found it all so funny that he let slip the cushion, which fell to the ground with a thud.

The cowherds laughed till their legs gave way; they laughed till the cows took fright. But the sage old men did not laugh. Their sad rheumy eyes looked down at the cushion and at Samba's large, masculine feet.

"So you think it is funny, do you, to make fun of your elders and betters? So you have no respect for the magic of our wisdom? Then with our wisdom of magic *we curse you!*" Their yellow eyes flashed and their gnarled fingers pointed at Samba. "May that woman's pestle of yours strike dead every young man in the tribe of Yadava!"

Laughter trailed away. The air was cold with the chill of the curse. The leaves on the trees shook.

Before the sage old men had limped out of sight, Samba had smashed the wooden pestle in two. The two halves he burned in the fire till they turned to ash, then he ground the ash into finest dust. Finally he sprinkled the dust into the sea, where it sank.

"There!" said Samba, brushing his hands together. "How shall the pestle kill us when there is no pestle?" And every man there breathed a sigh of relief. For though they did not fear to die, their insulting joke had put in danger the life of the Lord Krishna.

Down in the dark of the deep-fathomed sea, the powdered ash settled on the sand. Like seed it took root. Like seed it sprang up. Salt sea grasses grew, as straight and brittle as reeds of glass, and in among the stems swam the bright fish of the ocean.

Amid its own bubbling cloud of silver breath, a little fish nibbled the sea grasses, a crawling snail, a wriggling worm . . . and the silver hook inside that worm. With scarcely a struggle, the fish was pulled from the water by a fisherman, who carried it home in delight and ate it for supper with his family. No cowherd this fellow, for he loved the challenge of hunting — boar in the forest, lions in the hills, fish in the sea, and birds on the wing.

The cowherds of Yadava preferred to roast an ox, eat cheese from the creamery, and drink wine from the fruit in the orchards. Sitting on the beach at low tide, they celebrated their narrow escape, and laughed (as loud as they dared) at the thought of foiling that dreadful curse.

Everyone was there — Krishna, his brother Balarama, Samba, and all the Yadava cattlemen. The sea ebbed, but the wine flowed — heavy, heady wine. The brittle reeds on the shoreline tinkled like glass chimes in the breeze. The men drank in celebration — and the drink made them want to dance. The dancing made them thirsty, and so they drank some more. The drink made them thirstier — as thirsty as if they had drunk the salt sea — so they drank still more.

The ocean rolled, the drinkers reeled. The tide turned, and the mood of the drinkers turned too, from cheerfulness to surliness, from surliness to a fighting madness.

For no good reason, one pushed another. He rolled back in among the reeds, and one snapped off in his hand. He threw it like a spear, and it stabbed the young man in the throat. All at once a nonsensical quarrel turned into a frenzied battle. The lads took sides, the sides took arms — they broke off the sharp reeds and hurled them, with drunken lunges, blindly at one another. Balarama was pierced in the back, and the cold of the sages' curse chilled him to the marrow. "Go, Krishna! Get away!" he

89

called. Then he dragged himself into the shade of a tree and sat patiently, watching Death approach like a ship across the wide sea.

That poisonous curse cankered each graze, turned every cut into a deadly wound. By sunset, not a cowherd was left to call the cows to milking. Every one lay dead on the beach. The milkmaids watching for returning herds waited till night settled over them, and with it a sense of dread.

Krishna alone walked from the beach, his face full of anguish, his heart full of regret. He went deep into the forest, where the light was slight and green. Only the wind through the branches sounded the same as the sea. He thought back over his life — the women he had loved, the children he had cradled, the battles he had won. He thought about the vastness between the stars, the heat within the suns, the length of history and the shortness of life. Not another soul moved through the green shade of the forest.

None, that is, but the fisherman. He had left his fishing rod at home today and come in search of deer, with bow and arrow. His newest arrow hung at his side — the one tipped with sharpened fish bone cut from the remains of his fish dinner.

A movement, a shadowy shape. A deer?

The huntsman drew back his bow and fired, and Krishna, darling of the world, buckled his leg in pain. The arrow tip had pierced the sole of his foot, and the cold curse was already coursing through his veins.

So he laid his earthly life aside. Like a snake who sloughs off the papery glory of its skin to grow the greater, Krishna sloughed off his human form and returned to Heaven — a creature of spirit, a divine being once more, a radiance like the brightness left in your eye after looking at the sun.

The Lighthouse on the Lake

A JAPANESE LEGEND

THERE WAS once a lighthouse-keeper, tall and slender like his lighthouse and as dazzling to women as the light he tended. His name was Jimmu, and he sat in his high tower, feeling like the sun generously bestowing its beams on Lake Biwa.

A beautiful girl, Yuki, who lived on the shores of the lake, saw him out fishing one summer's day, and fell in love, as only a young girl can. Her soul, her life, her heart, her all, she placed in her father's boat, and rowed out to Jimmu. "I love you," she said.

Jimmu wound in his hook and attached another worm, looking at the girl. "Pretty little thing," he thought, and said, "I'm honored. But your parents will never allow us to meet. You're so young."

"I could row over the lake to your lighthouse after dark. My parents would never even know."

Jimmu was taken aback. It was such a very daring suggestion! The vast lake is a pretty place on a sunny day, but at night it is an eerie crevasse of gleaming dark between the looming Hira mountains. Yuki was certainly a remarkable girl if she was ready to cross the night lake. And how shameless! To suggest such a lover's tryst with a stranger, without a word about marriage. Jimmu was almost shocked . . . but pleasantly excited, too.

"Until tonight, then," he said, and her face filled with such joy that he congratulated himself on making her so happy.

That night, Yuki slipped from her bed and crept to the waterside. She launched her father's rowboat and unshipped the oars. Then, fixing her course by the lighthouse's shining beacon, she rowed toward her handsome lighthouse-keeper.

In her mind, she pictured happy days ahead: marriage, children, a little house like her parents' by the lakeshore, a garden in the shadow of the lighthouse . . . When the prow of the boat bumped the steps at the foot of the tall building, a smiling figure stood waiting with outstretched hand to help her ashore. She saw in Jimmu's smile everything she wanted to see: true love, a kind heart, a longing to share his whole life with her. She would help him trim the wick of his lamp, help him polish the mirrors in the lamp-room. She would cook the fish he caught in the lake each day, and bear him sons to work the lighthouse in his old age.

Night after night, Yuki visited her lover at the Hira lighthouse. No one ever knew. She rowed through sharp frost, her breath like smoke. She rowed through driving rain, her hair stuck to her like otter's fur. She rowed through summer lightning, when jagged forks jabbed at a meat-raw sky and tore it to shreds.

Jimmu marveled at her bravery, then he reveled in her love. He even mentioned marriage, in a vague sort of way — and almost meant it. After she was gone — rowing home before dawn could betray her secret — Jimmu would lie awake, looking at the haze of light around his lighthouse window, and wonder at his good fortune.

"She's better than any girl I ever met," he thought one August night, as he watched her little boat approach along the golden path of light. "Who else would do this for me? I shall marry her." The night was windy; the waves were higher than usual, and Yuki's progress was slow.

"Although, really, she ought to show more modesty."

The little boat pitched and Yuki's oars flailed like the legs of some water-borne insect.

"Perhaps she behaves like this with all the men — a flirt — a man-chaser!" thought Jimmu, ". . . although when would she have time to visit anyone else?"

Yuki stopped rowing to peel the wet hair away from her eyes.

"Perhaps she's mad with love for me because I'm so desirable," thought Jimmu. "No one else has ever rowed across the lake to cook me dinner." His wondering began to change to anxiety.

"Perhaps she's just mad," thought Jimmu. "I'd be mad myself, if I married a madwoman." Then came the worst possibility of all.

"Perhaps she's not a woman at all! Perhaps she's a demon sent to tempt me! Maybe she's an enchantress weaving an evil spell, even now, to trap me like a fly in a web! Yes! That's it! She's an evil spirit! A spirit of the lake!"

The heart which had felt so little real affection for Yuki experienced an unfamiliar pang of fright, a quiver of pure self-love. He must show the Powers of Evil that he was not a wicked man at all — no, not at all! He could resist temptation! He had no need of ghostly temptresses! The thought of Yuki's arms round his neck made him shiver with horror, now that his foolish imagination had convinced him she was a demon.

Leaping up the stairs to the lamp-room, he shielded his eyes against the brightness of the burning tallow wick and its mirrored reflections. His own shadow danced hugely against the wall. Jimmu snuffed out the flame with a leather bag, and coughed himself breathless in the acrid smoke.

Out on the lake, Yuki was plunged into total darkness. The golden path of light along which she had been rowing drowned in an instant, and left her blind. Gradually her eyes made out her own pale hands on the oars, the wet oars themselves, but beyond her oars' ends, nothing — blackness.

She was instantly lost. "Jimmu! Dearest! The light! The light has gone out! Jimmu! Trim the wick! I can't see the lighthouse! I can't see the shore!"

The darkness fell on her like a mudslide, stopping up her eyes and ears and nose and mouth. "Jimmu!" she tried to call, but the wind tore the words from her lips and repaid them with spray. One oar pulled free of its oarlock and drifted away from the boat. "Jimmu, help me! Shine a light! Call out to me! It's your own little Yuki! Why don't you hear me? Help me, Jimmu! I'm lost!"

In the lamp-room of the lighthouse, Jimmu sat with his hands over his ears, telling himself, "A demon would say anything to trick a man out of his soul!" He refused to hear. He shut his eyes and ears, and put out the flame of love in his heart as assuredly as he had snuffed out the wick.

Yuki went on calling. Though her little boat was filling with rain, though she had spun and drifted far out into the center of the lake, still she went on calling: "In the name of everything we mean to each other, light the light, Jimmu!"

When the second oar broke loose, she tried to retrieve it, leaning out too far. The boat capsized, and Yuki was plunged face-first into the icy black waves. As the cold soaked through her clothes, so the realization crept into her soul.

Jimmu had betrayed her. She saw, with terrible clarity, all that she had been too dazzled to see by lamplight: that Jimmu did not love her at all, had never loved her, cared nothing for her fate. She pulled herself carefully across the upturned boat, straddling the slimy keel.

"I curse you, Jimmu. Do you hear me now? I curse your lighthouse, and I curse you! I curse this lake that carried me to you, and I curse the mountains that looked on and did nothing to stop me! Disaster fall on you

as it fell on me the day I saw Jimmu the lighthouse-keeper!" Then she let go her grip on the keel and allowed herself to slide into the heaving lake, dropping like the lead on a fishing line directly to the bottom.

A jag of wind caught the empty boat and rolled it across the lake, smashing it against the base of the lighthouse. Another roused the waves to riot, foam crests seething into sudden life, ripping the crayfish pots from their tethers. The wind redoubled, pulling slates off the roof of Yuki's little house and branches off the shoreside trees. Out from behind the mountains came a twist of wind more ferocious than bears or mounted swordsmen. It raced across the lake, wrenching into the sky a million gallons of angry water.

The hurricane struck the lighthouse with wind and water, rubble and fish, wreckage and tree trunks and birds. It crazed the lamp-room like an eggshell, and tore the mortar from between the bricks. Trapped inside, Jimmu glimpsed the night sky through a hundred opening cracks. A moment later, the floor collapsed, and dropped him the height of the lighthouse as if down a deep, dark well.

Next day, nothing remained of the lighthouse on the shores of Lake Biwa. And now, each August, hurricanes spring from behind the mountains and lash the lake into a maelstrom, destroying, uprooting, demolishing the calm remains of summer. They come as regularly as a lover keeping a tryst with her sweetheart, but their twisting embrace is deadly, and, at heart, a whirling emptiness.

King Arthur Gives Back His Sword

A CELTIC LEGEND

LEGEND SPEAKS of a king who ruled when the world had need of heroes and taught men the nature of chivalry. His name was Arthur Pendragon and his kingdom was in the West. There was druid magic in his hands — a pure, white magic that gave him the strength to strike and the authority to govern. He carried the great sword Excalibur, and, by his side, its magic scabbard that protected the wearer from wounds.

He gathered around him a family of knights — good men (or well-intentioned, at least) — and made them swear to seek adventure and fight evil wherever they found it. To teach them humility, he seated them at a round table, giving no one pride of place, not even himself.

But knights are by nature competitive. They are trained from boyhood to win in the joust, to win in battle, to prove themselves the best. Equality and accord are not in the nature of knights. So rivalries, jealousies, petty differences broke out, which grew into feuds. The company of the Round Table began to split and splinter like a wheel embedded in a rut.

Open rebellion arose at last, led by Mordred, who drew to his side an army big and cruel enough to trample down a legion of angels. Arthur and his faithful knights prepared to fight the last great battle. They were hugely outnumbered, but by a rabble so grubbing, greedy, and unremarkable that they amounted to mere brass pennies — dozens needed to equal one silver knight.

Between tents fringed with blood, from daisy-eyed morning to sunflower noon, the two armies fought — cavalry charges like crashing surf, axes hammering out on shields the great drumbeat of war. The dark rabble of Mordred's infantry fell away, but the shining company of Arthur shrank, too. At last, only the black knight-champions of Mordred remained, and fought in single combat with the knights of the Round Table. Man by man they died, not one falling without his opponent paying the same price.

Finally, Arthur and Mordred met in the shadow of a castle wall, and a cry went up that silenced the rooks in the treetops. "All day I have pursued you, Mordred, and you have kept shifting ground. Are you afraid of dying or of damning your soul with treason by fighting your lawful king?"

"I am afraid of nothing," said Mordred, and the word "nothing" was in his mouth when Arthur's lance struck him a blow that shattered his armor like the ice on a lake. Looking down at the gaping wound in his chest, Mordred drew back his lips in a snarl. He pushed forward along the lance — as a boar will sometimes thrust onto the hunter's spear — and wielding his broadsword one last time, struck Arthur a blow that cracked his breastplate. "Die, Arthur Pendragon! Die and be forgotten!"

Impaled on the royal lance, Mordred died on his knees. Arthur fell backward into the arms of Sir Bedivere. "Where are my other knights?"

"I am all that is left, sire."

"What, only one? It is enough," whispered Arthur. "It takes only one man to tell the world: This is how it was, this is how it ended ... Lift me up."

"I'll fetch a stretcher — the women of the castle will help me carry you indoors. You can rest there. Get better . . ." said Bedivere.

"No. My time has come. Lift me on your back and carry me into that wood over there." The magic in Arthur's eyes could still command Bedivere's obedience. As Bedivere carried him, Arthur spoke despite his pain. "I have been here once before. When I was newly crowned, Merlin the Magician brought me here — to the shore of a lake in the middle of the forest. It was here that I was given Excalibur. It is entrusted to earthly kings only once in a thousand years, you know. It made me what I am."

"Your goodness and God's help made you that, my liege," said Bedivere, feeling tears cold on his cheeks.

"A witch stole the scabbard, or Mordred could not have wounded me today. But every man must die, Bedivere. Every man deserves to rest."

It grew dark, but still Bedivere plodded on through the wood, along a baffling maze of paths, carrying Arthur across his shoulders. Suddenly, a lake lay in front of him — an eye of light, mirroring the moon. Bedivere laid Arthur Pendragon down between the roots of an oak tree.

"I haven't the strength, Bedivere. Please — as a last act of friendship — return Excalibur to the lake for me . . ."

"Throw it in, you mean?" Sir Bedivere took the grand sword from Arthur's hip. He was exhausted himself and could barely carry it. It seemed a terrible waste of a sword, an ignoble and obscure end for the mighty Excalibur. So before he got to the lake, he hid the sword under some bracken and turned back toward his master.

"What did you see?" asked the King, pulling himself upright.

"See? Well, I . . . er . . . I saw the ripple stir the reeds, and moorhens hurrying away . . ."

"Liar!" said Arthur in a voice that turned Bedivere's blood to water. "Go back and do as I said!"

Bedivere turned and ran back to the sword. He *did* mean to throw it, he did almost throw it: twice he whirled it around his head. But then he thought of his task: to preserve the legend of Arthur and his knights, and keep the wonder and faith alive in the hearts of the people. How much easier it would be if he kept Excalibur for the world to see!

So he laid the sword down again on a cushion of moss, and went back to Arthur.

"What did you see?" asked the King.

"I saw a skein of geese and a shoal of fishes rise in a cloud of bubbles . . ."

"Traitor! Villain!" cried Arthur in a voice which turned Bedivere's blood to gall. Clutching the tree, trying to get up, he demanded, "Must I do it myself, after all?"

"No! No! I'll do it! I will!" Back through the trees Bedivere ran, in a frenzy of regret, thinking that the last words his king spoke to him would be in reproach. He snatched up the great sword, swung it three times around his head, staggering deep into the lake under the huge weight. Then he let it go, and it whirled about and about, a fragment of lightning, a sliver of moon.

In the center of the lake, just where the moon's reflection floated like a pallid face, an arm clad in white silk reached out of the water — a woman's arm, a woman's hand, but with strength enough to catch Excalibur by its hilt, brandish it three times, and draw it down into the lake.

Bedivere went back and told the King what he had seen. It seemed to pacify Arthur, to free him of his anxiety. A smile came to his lips, but he could barely speak any longer.

Suddenly, Bedivere heard behind him the splash of oars, and he ran to the waterside, thinking perhaps to glimpse the Lady of the Lake bearing Excalibur. But what he saw was a long, slender barge being rowed toward him by three veiled women in tissue-fine robes of gray. They beached the boat and moved ashore past Bedivere, lifting the King to his feet and leading him the short way to their craft. It seemed an easy journey for him, like a man walking to his own bed after a day's hard labor.

Just when Bedivere thought he was dreaming, the women spoke to him. "We are taking your lord to Avalon."

"Where he may rest and sleep and recover from the wounds of life."

"Do not mourn for him."

"How can I help but mourn?" said Bedivere. "The world will be lost without him."

"If there is ever a danger of the world being lost, young man," said the tallest of the women, "Arthur will come again, armed with the sword Excalibur. But for now, the world is not lost. Indeed, you saw it saved today from the forces of Evil. Don't forget that when you tell the history of Arthur, when you recount the legend of the Round Table."

The barge floated out from the shore, two women at the oars, the third cradling the King's head in her lap. He seemed to be asleep now, at rest, and the barge moved silently out across the lake, to be swallowed up by scarves of mist, curtains of diaphanous moonlight, hangings of velvet night.

A Bloodthirsty Tale

IT IS A STORY told all over the world. The Creator makes Humankind. Humankind disappoint their Creator. The Creator destroys what he has made. So it was with Re, in the days when he ruled both the world of people on earth as well as the family of gods in heaven.

"People are hatching plots against me! They are rebellious and disobedient. I don't know why I ever created them or any of their kind!" complained Re. "And yet . . ."

And yet Re was fond of his creation, and did not want to wipe people altogether off the face of the earth. A small punishment would serve, perhaps, to put the humans in their proper place, to teach them a lesson in humility.

So Re took the third eye from his forehead — the one that shone so brightly, as he sailed the Ship-of-a-Million-Days across heaven — his eye, the sun.

When Re wished (as now he wished), his eye took on the shape of a goddess, Hathor. Generally, Hathor was gentle and kind, but since the eye had bulged with fury as Re took it from his head, this time Hathor, too, was filled with furious rage. Snatching up a sword, she rushed out into the deserts, herding and chasing crowds of people ahead of her like flocks of frightened sheep. She laid about them with teeth and blade, killing and rending, till the human race cried aloud for the gods to pity them.

Only sunset put an end to the slaughter, when Hathor reported to Re in the Ship-of-a-Million-Days and was congratulated for her good work. Re reached out a hand to turn her back into his eye. "Return to me, O Powerful One. This day shall be remembered forever in the history of the world!"

But Hathor stepped out of reach. "Tomorrow I shall kill the rest!" she declared, laughing wildly. "The sands of the desert will turn red with their blood!" Her hands dripped blood, and she smeared it across her cheeks and hair like warpaint. "When I have finished my work, the history of people on earth will be at an end! I have tasted their blood, and I mean to drink every last drop!"

Re shuddered. "I've never seen her like this. She means to kill them all!" he realized with a pang of sorrow. He had not meant things to go so far. The people of earth were, after all, the flowers he had planted for a garden: he did not want them scythed down to the last bright petal.

"Quick!" he told his messengers. "Go to the Island of Elephantine, in the center of the Nile, and fetch me its bright red soil!" Crocodiles plunged into the river; cranes flew upstream. There, in the river, as scarlet as the back of the swimming hippopotamus god, lay the Island of Elephantine, rich in red ochre. It was smaller by half, after the messengers of Re had scoured away its soil.

"Quick! Quick!" Re told the High Priest of the temple at Memphis. "Pound this red earth to dust!"

"Quick! Quick! Quick!" he told the servant girls who worked in the fields. "Brew beer and ferment it with honey!"

All night, the priests pounded and the girls brewed. Then, just before
dawn, Re took the dusty dye and seven thousand pints of foaming beer,
and mixed the two together till they thickened and congealed into a
gleaming red liquor.

One jug at a time, Re poured out the thick red beer onto the ground.
Seven thousand jugs of oozing redness he poured out, until he and the
priests and the serving girls stood ankle-deep in it.

Then he sailed away in the Ship-of-a-Million-Days, as though the fate of the human race were of no concern to him.

Hathor, the eye of Re, woke from her slumbers and remembered her task for the day. She lifted her bloody sword and strode out into the world of people.

Splash, splash, splash, her feet waded into a lake of red. She looked around her and saw, as far as the eye could see, a quaggy mire of gore. "Indeed, I am the glory of Re that I spilled so much blood in a single day!" And in her bloodlust, she knelt down and drank what she mistook for the blood of Humankind.

She had not remembered it tasting so good! "If this is how the blood of my enemy tastes, then I shall kill and drink and drink and kill till the last mewling baby has paid for angering my master! Where are they hiding themselves? Let me root them out, these wretches! I, Hathor, am their doom!"

But after drinking a thousand jugs of the blood-red liquor, Hathor found she could not readily get to her feet to go after the remainder of Humankind. She could only manage to sit, with her feet dangling in the red lake, and drink a thousand jugs more.

Soon after, an unaccountable desire to sleep came over Hathor. She squinted up at the Ship-of-a-Million-Days, bearing the gods on high, but it seemed to be spinning about like an angry bluebottle fly. She watched it for as long as her eyes would stay open, then fell backward with a splash into the deepest, darkest drunken stupor the world has ever seen.

"Oooh, my head! Oh, my bursting head! Almighty Re, take pity on your servant! I'm not well!" When Hathor woke from her beery dreams, she could remember nothing about the day before. "How did I get here? What am I doing here? Where is the comfortable forehead of my master, Re? . . . And why do I feel so *ill*?"

Re helped her to her feet, cupped her affectionately in his hands and changed her back into his third eye, settling her in his forehead. Though she was very bloodshot for a while, and glowed less brightly, she was once again a solemn and sober eye who looked down kindly on the people of earth.

So, too, did Re, for having seen them come so close to destruction, he had learned to value them as among his best works of creation.

Rip Van Winkle

AN AMERICAN LEGEND

"WELL? You gonna feed the chickens, or what? D'you think that cow's gonna milk herself? S'pose you think sweeping the yard's beneath you! Mother told me it would be this way: me slaving my fingers to the bone and you laying up in bed, thinking you're the King of England!"

Rip Van Winkle rolled out of bed, but still his wife came after him, her bony hand pecking him through his nightshirt. It was five in the morning and today was turning out just like yesterday.

"And chop some wood if you're not too high and mighty! And mend that busted step before I fall down and kill myself. You'd like that, wouldn't you? Then you could drink alcohol and play skittles with those cheap friends of yours... And talking of that — I've told you till I'm blue — keep that flea-bitten dog of yours out of the house, will ya? Mother told me it would be this way. Marriage!"

Rip wished *his* mother had told him. He wished she had led him aside on his wedding day and said, "You don't want to do this, son. Here's a gun: go shoot yourself instead."

He got dressed, swept the yard, chopped wood, fed the chickens, and milked the cows. He cooked breakfast for his wife, picked the dog hairs off the rug, and made the beds. It was still only six o'clock and the day lay ahead of him like a pile of rocks.

As he mended the fence, his work took him farther and farther away from the house. The shouting grew fainter and fainter: *". . . And you let those slugs get to the cabbages again!"* Rip suddenly thought that if he walked way up the hill, he would not be able to hear it at all. His dog Bark looked at him, harassed and hangdog. "Let's go," said Rip. And they did.

He knew there would be heck to pay when he got home, but as he climbed between the red pine and maple trees and breathed the scent of the ferns, Rip hardly cared. He walked and walked, up the gorge, deep into the canyon, where the sound of falling water scrawled out every other sound. "Hear that, Bark? Peace. Perfect peace," he said.

Up past Sentry Bridge, Minnehaha Falls, and Frowning Cliff he climbed, where the sunlight barely trickled through the oaks but the stream plummeted down like silver mercury. And when he reached Rainbow Falls, he sat down among the braided colors of spray. He had never been so far up the glen before. Even his dog sat so still that white-tailed deer and stripy raccoons strolled by, unconcerned, and a chipmunk rolled among the moccasin flowers. At least, Rip thought it was a chipmunk at first.

Then he looked again and saw the hat, the clothes and little boots. And the barrel.

"Dang, blam, and fliminy bosh!" cursed the dwarf, as the barrel he had been pushing rolled away from him toward the brink of the falls. He pulled his hat right down, so as not to see it go.

Rip Van Winkle took two big strides and stopped the barrel with his foot. "Can I carry this some place for you?"

The dwarf pulled his hat off again and peered upward. "That's mighty

neighborly, sir, coming from a giant. My back's plumb busted trying to get it up the hill."

He led the way up a staircase of slippery black stones that led right behind the Rainbow Falls. Half-expecting to be washed away, Rip followed with the barrel, and Bark kept close to his heels. Behind the thunder of the waterfall, they found a little door, and behind the door, a great tavern — a cavern of a tavern, noisy with fifty or sixty dwarfs. By getting down on his hands and knees, Rip could just squeeze in through the door. Once inside, there was room for him to stand. At the sight of Rip, the dwarfs stopped stock-still and stared.

"He helped me with the keg!" explained the first dwarf.

"Swell, but who is he?

"What's he doing hereabouts?"

"Maybe he's dwarf-hunting." Their voices echoed around the cave, and when Bark trotted in, they cowered against the far wall.

"I'm Rip Van Winkle, and I'm . . . well, I'm hiding from my wife." (To his relief, there were no women dwarfs in sight.)

The dwarfs let out a single groan. "Oh, give the man a chair! Pour him a drink! Make room for the unfortunate fellow! Don't we know how it goes! *'Chop the wood! Hunt a rabbit! Fetch up the stores.'* Set that barrel down, Rip, and make yourself at home!"

Rip grinned shyly. "I'd better be getting back. She'll skin me alive if I don't do some chores."

But they all rushed at him, and slapped him on the bottom (because they could not reach his back), and hugged his legs, and tugged at his fingers. "Come and play skittles! You can be on our team!"

"That's not fair! We want him on our team!"

"You can have his dog on your team!"

"And you can have this mug of beer over your head!"

They squabbled and wrestled and giggled throughout the game. And though they lost three balls and broke a flower vase, nobody minded. Time and again, the little men helped themselves to ale from the barrel Rip had carried. "Have a cannikin yourself!" they kept saying, but Rip only ducked his head and said shyly, "Better not. The wife doesn't like me to touch strong drink."

At last, cheered on by his team, Rip scattered the skittles to the four corners of the cavern and five toppled out the door and over the water-fall.

"We win! We win! Our team wins! Bring the hero a drink!"

It was true, the game had given him a powerful thirst. The tankards were tiny; it couldn't hurt to sip just a thimbleful of ale ... The dwarfs set down a saucerful for Bark, the dog, as well.

At the first swallow, the cavern began to spin. At the second, everyone seemed to be standing on their heads. At the third, Bark seemed to be yawning and turning pink. Then darkness closed in on Rip Van Winkle from all sides.

"Of course. Human. We should have known."

"... not used to fairy beer ..."

"... too strong for him," said voices out of the darkness.

Then Rip fell asleep, and slept deeper than he had done ever since the day he first shared his big feather bed with his wife.

When he woke, there was no sign of the dwarfs. Bark's coat was re-markably dusty, but he woke when Rip patted him. Together they ducked out of the cave. The waterfall was tumbling just as before, the spray still spanning the gorge with rainbows, the white-tailed deer still grazing.

"Now we're for it," said Rip to his dog, as they tripped up the porch steps of his house. "Better mend that step this afternoon, I guess."

"Who are you?" said the woman at the door.

Rip was almost too startled to speak. "You're not my wife!"

"George! There's some old-fashioned hobo at the door, says I'm not his wife. George!"

"But I ... I ... I live here!"

"George! Says he lives here! You wanna fetch your gun?"

"But I ... Where's Mrs. Van Winkle?"

"Never heard of her. You got the wrong address."

"Sure you've heard of her, Mary," said the man who came out with his gun. "She was the old lady lived here before us. Husband disappeared. Lived here all alone. Fell down the step and broke her neck — she was old, mind."

Rip Van Winkle fell back a step or two. These people were not lying. The cow in the yard was not his cow. The axe on the woodpile was not his axe. Bark whimpered at the unfamiliar smells. "Disappeared, you say? Rip Van Winkle disappeared?"

The woman on the porch scratched her head. "Sure. Now George calls it back to my mind . . . disappeared 'bout fifty years back. Walked off one day into Watkins Glen, they say, and never came back. Folks said the fairies took him, but then folks would. Fell in the stream and drowned hisself, more like."

Now you might think that losing your farm, losing your feather bed, losing fifty years — and all in one day — might make a man a little bleak, unsettled, and resentful. But no. That was not the way it struck Rip Van Winkle. Rip Van Winkle could see a good side to most things. From the gate of his no-longer-home, he walked directly into town with his dog, sat down at the bar of the saloon, and told his story to anyone who would listen.

Within a fortnight, he was the toast of Finger Lake County.

The Raven and the Moon

AN ALASKAN MERIT MYTH

ONCE, when the night was too dark to bear, the fishing people of the north longed for some relief from the solid black sky and its cold hail of stars. What they did not realize was that a moon had been made for the hours of darkness, just as the sun had been made for day. But a miserly old man and his miserly young daughter, Loona, wanting to keep it for their own, had locked it away with their other treasures.

Now Raven, like the magpie, likes shiny things — stones, bones, buttons, and the like — and when he heard the two whispering one day about their secret hoard, he set his heart on having something out of that chest for his own collection of pretties.

There was no chance that Loona would ever marry: her father gave away nothing that was his, and Loona would never by choice leave the

114

house with its chest full of valuables. So instead of courting her, Raven, with a beat of his black wings, changed himself into two wing-shaped green leaves drooping from the bough of a waterside tree. When Loona came and sat on the bank to fish, the bough brushed her face, and the leaves fluttered into her mouth. She did not spit them out; they slipped easily down her throat and turned to a baby in her womb.

It was a little startling to find herself pregnant, but as she pointed out to her father, "Having a baby is like getting something for nothing."

Her old father agreed. "And now I need never share our pretties with any son-in-law."

So they made a crib out of furs, on rockers of whalebone, and when the child was born, laid it in the cradle. They called it Beaky, poor mite, because of its enormous hooked nose.

Beaky started to cry.

"Perhaps it's hungry," said Loona, and fed it. But still the baby cried.

"Perhaps it's wet," said her father, and turned over the furs in the cot. But still the baby cried.

"Perhaps it's cutting teeth," said Loona, and gave it her forefinger to mumble on. "Ouch! What a bite!" But still the baby cried.

"Perhaps it's sick," said the old man, and they took turns walking the baby up and down, up and down, up and down. But still it cried.

"Perhaps it's bored," said Loona. "It must have a toy to play with." So she made it a toy horse and a toy fish and sewed it a ball out of felt. But still the baby cried.

The old miser sank his head in his hands and his fingers in his ears. He needed his sleep. He longed for peace and quiet. But his home was full of bawling, the cries so piercing, so loud, that they seemed to lift the roof and split the plank walls of the hut. They took the baby outside and showed it the lap-lap of the sea and the big skua birds circling overhead. Beaky only hid his head under Loona's clothes and howled.

"We could always show it the moon," said the old man, his hair quite gray and his forehead puckered with misery. Loona thought for a moment and nodded.

Together they bolted the door, hung rugs over the windows, and dragged the chest into the center of the room. Loona scraped at the dirty floor and unearthed a large key. With it she unlocked the chest. Inside was another chest, and inside that was a large square box.

Inside the box was a wicker basket like a lobster pot, and inside the basket was a box shaped like a tube.

Inside the tube was a leather bag, and inside the leather bag was a sack.

Inside the sack was a bucket, and inside the bucket was a wooden pyramid.

Inside the pyramid was a smaller vellum container studded with stars. (Their shine was reflected in the beady black eyes of the watching baby.)

Inside the star-box was a bundle of orange cloth, and, shining through the cloth, a light so bright that all shadows were banished from the room. When Loona unwrapped the cloth, out across the floor rolled a glorious silver ball shining more brightly than any coin, brighter than any flame, brighter even than the stars.

At last, to their immense relief, the baby stopped crying. It clambered out of its crib, crawled across the floor and reached out.

Loona picked up the moon and threw it in the air playfully, to make Beaky laugh. "Higher! Higher!" chortled the baby.

The old man threw the shining ball higher still — almost as high as the smoke-hole in the center of the ceiling. "Higher! Higher!" cooed the baby, and flailed his little arms with joy.

Loona tossed the moon higher still, and all eyes were on the glittering treasure. So no one saw at what particular moment Raven recovered his true shape, put on black feathers and blacker beak, hunched his wings and scrabbled his claws among the ashes of the hearth.

Suddenly he sprang into the air, seized the moon in his beak, and flew with it once around the room, while Loona and her father chased him with outstretched hands. Then, with a flutter and a short cough amidst the smoke, Raven disappeared through the smoke-hole and into the night sky, carrying the moon in his beak.

Beneath him, the night shoreline was lit by moonlight for the first time.

The wave tips turned to silver, the stones on the beach glimmered, the fish scales scattered along the wharf glittered. Phosphorescent algae glowed in the rock pools.

Raven, greedy to add all these pretties to his collection, let go of the moon, which, instead of falling to earth, remained floating in the sky, out of reach of Loona, her father, or anyone else. It floated too high, at last, for even the circling skuas, though some greedy beak must surely slash away at its prettiness every month, for something pares the moon down to the tiniest sliver. Then, just when it seems to have been carried away entirely to some treasure-trove nest in the sky, there it is again, healing, growing, waxing big and white and beautiful.

Sir Patrick Spens

A SCOTTISH LEGEND

ALEXANDER, King of Scotland, sat in Dunfermline Town, drinking blood-red wine. His chair stood at the heart of a firelit room, the room at the heart of a castle. The rain outside could never wet the King's hair. The wind beat in vain against the castle walls. The courtiers loosened the fastenings of their velvet jackets and reveled in the warmth, the food, the dancing.

"Where are the men who will sail me a ship to Norway?" the King said.

"At this time of year, your majesty?"

"Why not? What's a little weather to one of *my* ships? I have betrothed my daughter Margaret to the Prince of Norway. But who shall have the honor of taking her to her marriage?"

An old knight sitting beside the King, half-asleep and remembering summer days, mumbled, "Well, of course, Sir Patrick Spens is the best sea captain in all Scotland." So the King wrote a letter commanding Sir Patrick to set sail the next day.

When the letter reached him he was walking on the beach, his gray hair tangled with the salt wind. As he read, he laughed out loud. "Is this a joke? No one puts to sea at this time of year!"

The King's messenger neither answered nor looked him in the eye. Then Spens knew that the letter was in earnest. Deathly pale, the letter crumpling in his hand, he turned back toward the harbor. The gray sea wall curved like a beckoning arm.

He thrust his head in at the lighted door of the inn and bellowed for his crew. "Make ready the King's ship! Men to the rigging! Men to the sheets! We sail today for Norway with the King's daughter for cargo!"

His first mate pursued him out into the cold and caught him by the sleeve. "You don't mean it, Captain! You'll never sail today! Last night the new moon held the old in her crescent: There'll be a storm before noon, or I never read the weather in a sailor's sky!"

Spens narrowed his eyes and looked out to sea, as if he could read more than the weather in the cursive waves. "I saw it too, old friend, but the King's command is our duty."

A crowd of rowdy courtiers tripped and trotted down the jetty, holding on to their hats and whinnying excitedly. They thought it would be jolly to accompany the Princess Margaret. "Oh, look now!" said one, mincing up the gangplank. "I've wetted my new cork-heeled shoes!" Bright silk handkerchiefs fluttered on the jetty, as ladies waved goodbye to their pretty beaux.

It was only a short voyage. They reached Norway in safety, and delivered the Princess up to strangers and foreigners. Then Sir Patrick Spens and his cargo of courtiers turned back for Scotland.

At that time of year, storms prowl the Firth of Forth like winter wolves, seeking ships to devour. Only a short voyage, but the longest any man ever makes. The wind plucked off the sails like petals from a flower, and broke the mast like a green stalk. Waves rose up as high as the walls of

Dunfermline Castle, and fell on the ship like stone. Out of the noise and frenzy of the storm they sailed, down, down into green silence, down, down into black cold, down, down to where the weed beckons and the fishes kiss.

That new moon has waxed and waned many times since the ladies waved goodbye to their beaux. But come moon, go moon, they will never meet again. For the courtiers are at the bottom of the sea, ranged at the feet of Scotland's finest sea captain. Only their cork-heeled shoes and fine-feathered hats float like sea birds on the sea's shining swell.

The Saltcellar

A SCANDINAVIAN MYTH

IN THE DAYS when the sea was sweet (though the people around it were no sweeter than now), the King of Denmark visited the King of Sweden.

"Denmark salutes you!" said King Frodi. "May you live a thousand years!"

"Thank you," said King Fiolnir. "Sweden welcomes King Frodi. May your fame fill the ear of the world as the sea fills a seashell ... Now, let's eat, and you can tell me why you've come."

King Frodi and King Fiolnir linked arms and walked in to dinner. All through the meal, Frodi eyed the two girls who brought him his food — big, strapping Swedish girls with braids as long as bell-ropes and muscles like bell-ringers. "I hear they pull men like wishbones," he said wistfully to King Fiolnir.

"Were you looking for a wife, perhaps?" asked Fiolnir politely.

121

"Good heavens, no! We have plenty of *pretty* women in Denmark. No, I'm looking for two strong sla . . . workers," said Frodi mysteriously. "I have . . . I have some work that needs to be done."

"Then you shall have Fenia and Menia!" declared King Fiolnir. He would be sorry to lose the girls, but hospitality demanded he should give his visitor what he most desired.

Fenia and Menia were women you could moor a boat to with an easy mind. Their knees were as big as capstans and their braids hung like ships' hawsers past shoulders like harbor breakwaters. They were jolly, willing workers, too. King Frodi accepted them eagerly and took them home — the prize he had sought far and wide.

For at home in Denmark, King Frodi had a mill, and now he had someone to turn it.

The mill had been given him by the King of Giants, two round stones balanced one on the other like twin pillows of rock. But they were so huge that no one in all Denmark had been able to move the grindstones around. What a reward awaited Frodi, now that Fenia and Menia could make the stones turn! For it was a magic mill: from between its bulging grindstones poured whatever was asked of it.

Frodi asked for gold, and the girls turned the treadwheel, and the mill ground gold dust.

Frodi asked for peace, and the girls turned the treadwheel, and the mill ground peace.

Frodi asked for happiness for all of Denmark. But he never gave a thought to Fenia and Menia, who turned the magic mill. He chained them to the treadwheel, and day and night they worked.

"When may we rest?" asked the millers, toiling around their wheel.

"When the cuckoo stops singing," said Frodi, feeling the gold dust run through his fingers.

"But the cuckoo sings day and night. When may we sleep?" asked the giant millers, walking their wheel.

"Only while you are singing," said Frodi, and laughed to see the barrels filling up with peace.

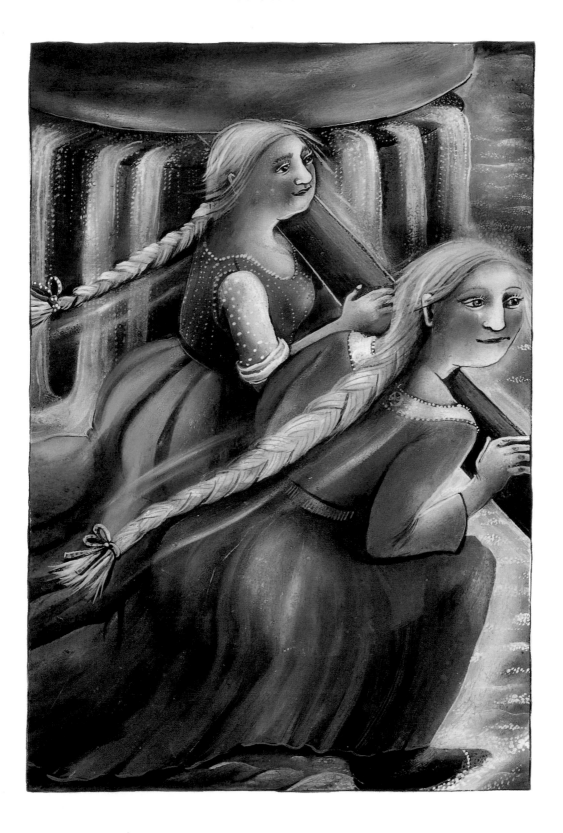

Fenia and Menia could not sleep while they sang, as Frodi well knew, but then Frodi did not know that they could sing at all. He certainly did not know that Fenia and Menia could sing magic songs. "Sleep while you're singing," said Frodi unkindly, so the sisters began to sing a song in their own mellifluous language:

> "Come some army with millions of horses;
> Come some army with myriads of men;
> Come some fleet with battalions of pirates,
> And kill this king who has chained us here!
>
> Come you foes of dirty Denmark;
> Come you foes of Frodi King.
> Come you foes of peace and prosperity,
> And kill this man who has made us slaves!"

That very night, despite the barrels of peace piled around Frodi's palace, pirates came raging up the rocky shore. A sea-king called Mysing and an army of mermen killed Frodi in his treasure-house, and left him head-down in a barrel of peace.

They stole the mill and they stole its millers. They stole the treadwheel and they stole the gold. They carried them all onto their flagship and put out to sea before Denmark even woke.

"Welcome aboard, sweet maidens!" said Mysing, smiling.

"You have set us free!" said Fenia. "We can breathe again!"

"We can see the sky," said Menia, "and feel the starlight running down our hair!" And they danced on deck as the ship crossed the bar.

"Grind, sweet maidens," said Mysing, smiling.

"For our rescuers? Anything! Name it!" said the girls.

"Grind me out *salt*," said Mysing, smiling. "Fine white salt, more precious than gold. For I am a salt merchant and sell rare salt to the kings of the world, to flavor their royal meat."

"Fine white salt for the sea-king Mysing!" sang Fenia and Menia, skipping around their wheel. "Fine white salt for the tables of royalty!" and the salt poured down into the holds below.

On and on till midnight Fenia and Menia trotted around the treadwheel, grinding. The moon rose up as white as salt and the Dog Star licked it. Then the ship's brass bell rang midnight.

"Time to rest," said Fenia and Menia. "More salt tomorrow, but now we are sleepy."

"Grind more salt!" said Mysing, and lashed shut the door with anchor chains. "You'll stop when I say, and not before!"

Fenia looked at Menia. Life had not been fair. Workers in Sweden, slaves in Denmark, and now captives even on the sweet free-running sea. "Let's grind out salt, then," they said to each other. "Enough and more than our dear master Mysing wants."

They ground out salt till the holds were full.

Then they ground out more, even when Mysing thanked them and asked them to stop.

They ground out salt while the crew was sleeping, and they ground out salt till the sun came up. The sun lit a ship blizzard-white with salt.

Mounds rounded the decks, dunes buried the bridge, and the ship wallowed as low as a basking whale.

"Stop! Stop! *Stop!*" screamed Mysing for the thousandth time, ladling salt overboard with his two hands. But Fenia and Menia went on working.

Still the salt poured from the magic mill, stifling the mermen in their hammocks. Still Fenia and Menia skipped around their treadwheel, making more salt than ever Mysing had carried over the sea.

At last, with a groan, the overladen ship dipped its prow beneath the waves. Mysing, who was halfway up the mast, climbing up toward the sky, saw his precious cargo of salt turn transparent under the first green flood. Then his ship fell away from under him, into the deep sweet ocean.

The might of the sea and the strong sea tides are still turning the magic mill. Like a prayer wheel it revolves in the sea's dark cellars, making salt. If it had been grinding peace when the ship sank, there might be fewer wars. If it had been grinding gold, then sailors would all be as rich as emperors. But the mill was grinding salt when it sank to the sea's cellars, and it has ground out salt now for a thousand years and more.

That is why the seas are salty and all salt merchants poor. None is poorer than Mysing, however, who lies trapped beneath the millstones, his bones ground down and his soul salt-corroded away.

As for Fenia and Menia, they escaped from the treadwheel as it rolled along the sea bed, struck out for the surface, and swam for home. Their knees were like capstans and their braids ships' hawsers, and their shoulders as big as harbor breakwaters. So it may well be that they reached dry land, where they pulled more men like wishbones, or sang magic songs, and savored the salty starlight running down their golden hair.

About the Stories

The Silver-Miners   *1*

Bolivians enjoy an almost personal relationship with the landscape that surrounds them. I am indebted to M. Rigoberto Paredes and his book *Mitos, Supersticiones y Supervivencias Populares de Bolivia* for the contents of this story.

The Men in the Moon   *6*

The Chaga people of Kenya display, in this story, a unique concept of the moon being attached to the earth by a causeway.

Dream Journey   *14*

The dangers, frustrations, and responsibilities of leadership are a large aspect of this Maori story about an exceptionally enlightened chief.

Roland and the Horn Olivant   *20*

In AD 778, Basque warriors annihilated the rearguard of Charlemagne's retreating army. As the story was retold, Saracens were substituted for the Basques. The epic poem *Chanson de Roland*, recounting Roland's heroic last stand, was written in the early twelfth century.

A Question of Life and Death   *27*

During the fourth century BC, The Boeotian city of Thebes was briefly the leading power base within the Greek Empire. Sophocles wrote a play about Oedipus, a legendary king of Thebes — a sorry tale from start to finish, but for his defeat of the Sphinx.

The Harp of Dagda   *31*

The Dagda, or Daghdha, was the Irish "good god" or "great father," "The Mighty One of Great Knowledge". He could kill and restore life with his giant club, and had control over harvests and the weather. His worship was prevalent around 200 BC.

A Nest and a Web *38*

In AD 622, Muhammad moved from Mecca to Medina, on a journey now called the Hejira or migration. It marks year one of the Muslim calendar. This is a story told about that journey.

Ash *42*

This is a shortened retelling of the life and feats of strength of Duktuthl, or "Dirty Skin," told by the Tlingit tribe inhabiting the northwest coast of North America.

The Tower of Babel *51*

The plain where the tower was said to have been built is the Tigris-Euphrates basin where Mesopotamian civilizations erected ziggurat temples as gateways to Heaven. It was originally told, not as a warning against pride and ambition, but simply to explain the origin of languages.

Saint Christopher *53*

"Thou hast borne all the world upon thee, and its sins likewise," says the child to Christopher in an antique English telling of the traditional European tale. Dr. Brewer in *Myth and Legend* writes, "This is an allegory: Christopher means Christbearer; the child was Christ, and the river was the river of death."

God Moves Away *57*

Togo is one of the smallest countries in Africa, sandwiched between Ghana and Benin, in the west. Its chief crop is maize, so it is no surprise that the pounding of maize with pestle and mortar features in its myths.

Wilhelm Tell *60*

It has never been possible to track down a real-life figure on whom Wilhelm Tell might be based. He seems to be a fifteenth-century invention, exactly mirroring the Norse *Saga of Thidrek* in which Egil the Archer shoots an apple off his son's head.

A HEART OF STONE *70*

The Greek myth of Pygmalion, as told in the Latin poet Ovid's *Metamorphoses*, was the basis for George Bernard Shaw's modern comedy, *Pygmalion*, and thus for the musical *My Fair Lady*. Aphrodite was the Greek goddess of love; Ovid used the name of Venus, her Roman equivalent.

BABUSHKA *75*

"Babushka" simply means "grandmother" in Russian, and is used of any old peasant lady. She is the Russian equivalent of Saint Nicholas, her poignant story explaining the tradition of giving presents to children at Christmas.

THE PIG GOES COURTING *81*

Kamapua'a's name means "hog child," and his hilarious mythology largely explains features of Hawaiian geology and natural phenomena. He is impulsive and unpredictable — a good friend to have around, but something of a liability, too.

CAN KRISHNA DIE? *86*

Though Krishna's name means "the black one," he is usually depicted as having a blue face of ineffable beauty. He is featured in the ancient Hindu text *The Bhagavad-Gita*, as an avatar (or incarnation) of the god Vishnu.

THE LIGHTHOUSE ON THE LAKE *91*

The hurricanes which frequently rage across Japan's Lake Biwa in August are called Hira hurricanes, because they blow from the Hira mountain range. The myth of the lighthouse-keeper is an attempt to explain this seasonal cataclysm.

KING ARTHUR GIVES BACK HIS SWORD *98*

The ninth-century *Historia Britonum* mentions a warlord called Arthur leading the Saxons in twelve battles culminating in a triumphant victory in about 500 BC. The Arthurian tradition has little to do with him, however, and grew up during the Age of Chivalry (the twelfth and thirteenth centuries), combining Celtic legend and Christian allegory.

A BLOODTHIRSTY TALE   *103*

Hathor, benign and gentle goddess of Egyptian mythology, was also the fearful Sekhmet — Powerful One. On her feast day, the preparation of strong drink was entrusted to girls instead of men, and toasts drunk to the goddess. She thus became the goddess of wine.

RIP VAN WINKLE   *108*

American writer Washington Irving gave him a name, in his *The Sketch Book of Geoffrey Crayon, Gent.* But Rip Van Winkle existed long before that, in legend and rumor, in the Catskill Mountains of New York State.

THE RAVEN AND THE MOON   *114*

There are many variants of this story. Its original function was to explain why the moon waxes and wanes. Raven is the Alaskan Merit animal of creation, responsible for making the world and unearthing the sun from the ground.

SIR PATRICK SPENS   *118*

In AD 1266 Norway renounced claims on the Hebrides Islands in return for a marriage between Prince Eric of Norway and Princess Margaret of Scotland. In 1281 the Princess embarked for Norway and her wedding. On the return trip, a terrible storm sank the ship that had carried her.

THE SALTCELLAR   *121*

The many variants of this worldwide myth have littered the sea bed with mills and cellars, all churning out salt. This version is Scandinavian. Though it may seem odd for the pirates to rate salt a precious cargo, it was once a vital and priceless food preservative.